REGAINING OUR BALANCE

Rediscovering Paradox and Distinctions

Kent Groethe

© Kent Groethe, 2005

ISBN 0-9768365-8-0

All rights reserved. No part of this book may be reproduced in any form without written permission from the author.

All Scripture quotations, unless otherwise indicated, are taken from the Holy Bible, New International Version®. NIV®.
Copyrights © 1973, 1978, 1984 by International Bible Society.
Used by permission of Zondervan Publishing House. All rights reserved.

Printed in the United States of America.

Edit/Format by Minion Editing.   www.joyminion.com

Bible Alive Ministries
P.O. Box 372
Fergus Falls, MN 56538

Email: biblealiveministries@yahoo.com or kentgroethe@gmail.com

Website: www.bible-aliveministries.com

CONTENTS

Preface 4

Introduction 7

Distinction 1 13
Salvation: Faith and Baptism

Distinction 2 28
Grace: Common and Saving

Distinction 3 35
The Word: Law and Gospel

Distinction 4 44
Language: Technical and Psychological

Paradox 1 54
God: Three in One

Paradox 2 61
Jesus: God and Man

Paradox 3 65
Christian: Saint and Sinner

Conclusion 73

Notes 75

PREFACE

This work is a critique of my denomination, the Evangelical Lutheran Church in America (ELCA). It is my assessment as a pastor in this denomination. I must admit that the motivation for this writing is to expose what I perceive to be common errors in theology of our clergy. These errors are ultimately manifested in the ministry of particular congregations and negatively affect the true proclamation of the Gospel.

I do not attempt to explore various trends in thinking or common theological positions of theologians in our church colleges and seminaries, nor do I seek to make judgments about the theological positions of our church-wide leaders in Chicago. That task would be highly speculative and presumptuous. Instead, I will discuss current theological trends and beliefs in my world: among Lutheran pastors in eastern North Dakota and northern Minnesota. The following reflections spring from countless conversations about Lutheran doctrine that I have had with my colleagues over the past sixteen years. These issues also arise from the frustrations and concerns I have heard repeated time and again from our lay people regarding the theological conclusions of many pastors.

I undertake this enterprise with fear, trembling and great humility. It is so easy to criticize, and to find fault gives one a certain warped kind of pleasure. As I raise my finger to point out possible errors in others' thinking, I am all too conscious that at any given moment I also may be holding theological perspectives and opinions that are distorted, based less on Scripture and the church's confessions and more on my own prejudices and faulty thinking.

The only reason I attempt such an endeavor is that I am part of a denomination which is deliberately "confessional;" that is, it acknowledges that we as individuals and as communities of faith are so biased by our present environment and the age we live in that we need the help of Christians throughout the centuries to help us understand God and the Scriptures accurately. I speak not to give my personal opinion concerning theological musings but to express my opinion regarding what the Lutheran Church has said about certain matters from the beginning.

At this point I must also confess my sin. I have all too often criticized those clergy whose theological opinions or beliefs differ from my own or that I believed were false or mistaken; regretfully, I have usually been critical behind their backs. I have gathered all too often with like-minded pastors and laughed at the clergy who were on the opposite side of theological issues. I have labeled many colleagues as "liberal," "non-confessional" and "un-Biblical" without giving them the chance to explain themselves more fully. I have often joyfully joined the criticism of members of my congregations and other pastors with my own theological bent in discarding the ELCA wholesale because of perceived errors in thinking among a portion.

I want to change. I want to express my thoughts and concerns personally to those with whom I disagree. I am committed to listening carefully to the "other side" in an attempt to hear their position accurately, and to learn something. Imagine that! I believe that the less our ideas and positions are laid out publicly for all to hear and argue against, the more our thoughts will remain weak and lack integrity. I hereby vow to love my theological opponents as Christ loves us, regardless of our individual opinions on the details of theology. I also promise to be bold and uncompromising when I am confronted with theology that I believe is wrong and harmful to the mission and ministry of the church. I will speak my thoughts in love, even though they may be baptized in passion.

What are my goals? The first is personal. I want to critique openly and publicly instead of secretly and privately. I trust that this process will help exorcise the demons of my judgmentalism. It is a difficult task because I want to be accepted and liked by my colleagues; by honestly sharing my differences, I run the risk of possibly losing their acceptance and friendship. I do this because I trust that the majority of those who read this will respect my arguments – if not my conclusions.

My other reason for this endeavor is that I want my beliefs and perspectives to be challenged and attacked (in love) so they can be tested and altered where and when needed. I admit there is a great limitation to my ability to think and to know truth. I am encumbered on my journey with a very narrow view of the world and of God as a result of the peculiarities of my life. I am a twentieth-century, middle-class American male with many unconscious motivations which cause me to think one way over another. In other words, I need help to see clearly. I need my ideas to be challenged by others who may see certain things more clearly or from a better perspective. If my thoughts are true, I need not fear that they will collapse because of scrutiny and a public hearing. If my thoughts are faulty, then I welcome correction. All I ask is that our dialogue be undergirded with the presupposition that the Scriptures and the Lutheran confessions are indeed a faithful expression of Christian truth.

It is my hope that this work will stimulate honest and genuine conversation in our church between people with differing ideas, and that this could be done in love. May truth, not personal glory or satisfaction, be our objective. May we glorify our Lord and God by an accurate proclamation of the Gospel and reach the world with the good news of Jesus Christ.

INTRODUCTION

One beautiful summer afternoon about eight years ago, my Pentecostal brother Craig and I were fishing on Crystal Lake near Pelican Rapids, Minnesota. Fishing was not the top priority of the day, however. As usual, we were consumed in theological debate. Fishing was merely an afterthought.

The topic of the day was the paradoxical nature of most theological conclusions and the penchant for individuals to miss the paradox. We talked about the truths of God being both one and three, Jesus being both God and man, humans being both saints and sinners, the kingdom of God being both an 'already' and a 'not yet' experience, communion elements being both bread/wine and body/blood, and other examples of paradox.

Our conversation was interrupted when there was a tug at the other end of Craig's fishing line. "I got a fish!" he exclaimed as he quickly turned his attention to reeling in his prize. After a few moments he experienced a constant tug which told him that we had trolled through some weeds and that he had snagged one. "No, I guess it's a weed," he concluded as he lost his enthusiasm for reeling in the line.

Jokingly, I said, "There you go, assuming that something is either one thing or another. You forgot a third option; that you have both a fish and a weed." I was merely trying to add a little humor to our much-too-serious discussion on paradoxes.

When Craig had almost reeled in the entire line, we saw a long green weed float to the surface. As he grabbed the line with one hand to pull the weed off his hook, we were surprised to see a small northern pike wiggling on the end. We laughed at the epiphany and were struck by the fact that God had entered our discussion Himself to add an exclamation point with this object lesson. While we were talking about people having a hard time thinking in *both/and* terms, God reminded us that we were not exempt from such tendencies ourselves.

Even though I perceive distorted thinking among clergy on a variety of theological issues, I believe that most of it has one common root: a loss of paradoxical thinking and sloppiness in regard to making distinctions.

Theological truth is most often only accurately understood in the marriage of two seemingly contradictory notions. At the same time, errors often occur in theological reflection when we fail to see that certain issues need to be parsed. For instance, in understanding grace, mistakes are made when one does not distinguish between a general grace that God gives to all and the grace that justifies but is received only through specific means. One of the greatest gifts Lutheranism has for the larger church family is the uncompromising adherence to the mystery of the paradox and the invaluable tool of carefully distinguishing parts of a theological issue. However, many clergy unwittingly fail to understand the reality of essential paradoxes and distinctions in their theological reflections.

More and more Lutheran pastors are focusing on half of the paradox or missing subtle distinctions which are necessary for right theology. For instance, the Gospel defended to the exclusion of the law, focus placed on the head to the exclusion of the heart, baptism emphasized over faith, the great commandment stressed over the great commission, technical language used instead of psychological, general grace undistinguished from saving grace and so on. By no means is this happening in every quarter nor by every pastor. Yet, it is prevalent enough to make the entire church unbalanced and ineffective in sharing God's Word in a way that transforms lives.

This one-sided stance has several causes. One is a reaction against perceived abuses of theology by the "evangelical" or fundamentalist communities of faith. Because we have examples of Christians abandoning the law/Gospel dichotomy and focusing too heavily on the law, many Lutheran clergy have abandoned a both/and stance in order to focus more on the Gospel in order to counter legalism. Or, we are tempted to abandon talk about personal faith and instead emphasize baptism in order to escape the dangers of teaching only the necessity of making a subjective decision. We fear the self-righteousness and privatization of faith, which we assume is taking place through popular Christianity that often seems to influence our people more than Lutheran doctrine. We tend to overemphasize the head aspect of faith to the exclusion of a heart experience and the objective over the subjective, because we have witnessed many lay people who have succumbed to an unhealthy emotionalism stemming from a charismatic or "conversion" experience.

Besides seeking to counter an opposite extreme, another reason we often lose sight of the paradox is because it is unnatural for us to think in both/and categories. When my brother Craig and I were fishing, it was easy to assume that truth was either one thing or another. Distinctions also are easy to miss because we naturally assume that life, as well as theology, is more simple or black-and-white than it really is.

Paradox means that two different and seemingly contradictory truths can both be correct. The nature of paradox is that when one tries to build theological or philosophical truths around one of two paradoxical truths while ignoring the other, conclusions will be skewed and corrupted. For instance, one paradox is the reality of both the humanity and the divinity of Jesus Christ. Jehovah's Witnesses accept Jesus' humanity while rejecting His divinity. Everything they say about Jesus' humanity is true. If one sits and listens to them, one will not be able to refute their arguments in this regard. The Christian can only nod in agreement when the Jehovah's Witnesses speak of Jesus' crying, bleeding, hurting, feeling and dying. They are articulating truth. However, when they began to assert other theological conclusions based on this reality without considering Jesus' divinity at the same time, they err. Here is a case where two truths make a truth, but one of the truths separated from the paradoxical other often makes an untruth.

This might be similar to the medallion in the fiction movie, *Raiders of the Lost Ark*. The setting is the 1930s and the Nazis are looking for the Ark of the Covenant which carried the Ten Commandments and accompanied the Israelites of the Old Testament. They had strong evidence that it was last deposited in a particular near-eastern town that was now hidden under centuries of sand and earth. Once they located the site of the old city, they began a massive archeological dig hoping to locate the precious Ark.

The task of uncovering the entire city would have taken years, and the Nazis were too impatient to wait that long. There was a shortcut, however. One of the first buildings the Nazis uncovered had a room containing a miniature model of the original city. In the roof of that room was a circular opening leading to the outside. On the floor in the center of the room was a hole where the staff of the Bible character Aaron was to be placed. If a particular medallion was placed on top of the staff at the right time of day, sunlight would enter the room and pierce through a small hole in the center of the medallion. The light would then be projected onto the model of the city and shine on the location where the Ark of the Covenant could be found.

Consequently, the Nazis needed to locate the medallion before they could proceed because it gave the height of Aaron's original staff. Only the exact-sized staff would accurately focus the light onto the correct spot on the miniature city. The Nazis discovered that the medallion was in the hands of the daughter of an archeologist who owned a tavern in the mountains of Tibet. Meanwhile, the good guy, Indiana Jones, also discovered the location of this key to finding the ark. Both parties converged upon the tavern on the same evening, and as they fought it out, a fire was started. The medallion, which had been casually draped over the centerpiece on a certain table, was spotted by the leader of the Nazi group as the fight continued. As he grabbed it, he painfully discovered that it was red hot from the flames. Screaming in pain, he ran outside to bury his burned hand in the snow.

Indiana Jones ended up winning the battle and possessing the precious medallion with its all-important height measurement of Aaron's staff. The Nazi leader was thrilled to discover that he, too, had the measurement because the impression of one side of the medallion had seared into his hand. Elated, the Nazis made their staff the height given by that side of the medallion. They also constructed another medallion based on the size of the mark on the seared hand. They lost no time setting the staff up in the room with the miniature city and placed the medallion on top. When the sun hit the center hole of the medallion, a ray of light shone on the model city and revealed where they should be digging. They began focusing their digging in that location.

There was one problem. The other side of the medallion, which the Nazis did not have, had further instructions stating that one should subtract a certain amount of height from the height given on the opposite side. This meant that the Nazis were wasting their time by digging in the wrong location. Both sides of the medallion were needed to gain enough information to accurately know where to look. One side led only to errors in calculations.

This is similar to how a paradox works. Errors in thinking can ensue when both truths of a paradox are not held in tension. I often encounter colleagues who are proceeding with deeper theological reflection while clinging to only one facet of a paradox. As a result, they are often making serious errors in their conclusions about faith. These false conclusions often have profound ramifications for the teaching of the Gospel. For example, consider the paradox of Gospel/law. Those who proclaim the Gospel, but do not take the law seriously because they think the two are in conflict, often reach theological conclusions that are false. They use the Gospel as the only springboard into greater theological reflection, rather than the paradox as a whole. Gospel-only clergy can easily end up with a universal salvation that can hinder or stop their invitation for members to come to faith as well as kill mission outreach.

Distinctions, in many ways, are the opposite of paradoxes. While paradox demands us to carry two truths that are in tension together into our theological reflection, distinction demands that we parse certain truths (or at least statements concerning truth) because the same statement may be true in certain cases but false in others.

For example, I have been an avid runner since high school, even self-righteously so. Imagine my consternation when a family member said, "Walking is as good for you as running." I was insulted and went on the defensive. I was sure that running was superior. Unfortunately for my position, my relative was a nurse. She cited medical studies to prove her point. This statement of hers bothered me for some time, until I realized that distinctions needed to be made: walking is better for the joints and legs than running; walking is as good as running for burning calories, if one goes the same distance; but walking is *not* as good as running in regard to cardio-vascular conditioning.

We are often sloppy in our use of statements of truth, and many times fail to distinguish in what ways a statement is true and in what ways it is false. This happens in everyday speech, and it happens in theology.

The goals of this work are to address common distinctions and paradoxes upon which orthodox Christianity has always depended and to argue that too many clergy are failing to be guided by these faithful tools. The first part of this work will look at four common distinctions, and the second part will identify three paradoxes vital for proper theology.

Inner ear infections affect how one walks. I often have parishioners in the hospital because the infection brings with it dizziness and loss of balance, both of which could be dangerous. Something similar has happened to our church. We have an "ear problem" that has caused theological imbalance. We have failed to hear the whole of Scriptural truth and the Lutheran confessions, and have instead picked and chosen only those parts that appeal to us. This has caused us often to miss the paradox or to ignore important distinctions. As a result, our witness for Jesus Christ often loses the power of God that comes when the Word is spoken clearly and accurately. My goal is that I could somehow be a catalyst for a renewed embrace of the distinctions and paradoxes so that our church might regain her balance.

DISTINCTION 1

Salvation: Baptism and Faith

Mark 16:16 states "Whoever believes and is baptized will be saved." Through the centuries, the Christian church has continued to affirm the need for both baptism and faith for an individual to experience salvation. Here, both the objective (baptism) and the subjective (faith) aspects of entering the kingdom are expressed. God's bold initiative and action through Jesus Christ upon blind and dead sinners are linked to the waters of baptism. Human response (albeit only with the aid of the Holy Spirit) is linked to faith.

The temptation for Lutheran clergy is to emphasize baptism at the expense of faith. In fact, faith is often seen as an enemy to the truth that humans cannot cooperate in any way in the saving process. Many Lutheran clergy with whom I have conversed on this topic seem to consider faith as some sort of work (at least possibly perceived as such by lay people), and thus a threat to the notion that God does everything in the conversion process.

Baptism has been elevated among many clergy to the point that any response by the human seems at odds with the image of God accepting a helpless infant into His family without an iota of response whatsoever. As a result, faith is often neglected in preaching and teaching, and a call for response is regarded as heretical. This de-emphasis on faith is the result of both a misunderstanding of what faith is as well as a conscious effort to counter the perceived errors of evangelicals and fundamentalists who often emphasize faith and human response at the expense of baptism and God's work in the saving process.

In many quarters of our church, the phrases "the priesthood of all believers" and "the ministry of believers" have been altered to "the priesthood of all the baptized" and the "ministry of the baptized." At first glance, the changes may seem harmless. But the changes encourage us to think that salvation is completed in baptism and that all baptized people make up the church. The existence of faith in a baptized member is not even addressed. People without faith are told to serve God in the world because they have been baptized. What then happens is a leap-frogging from baptism over faith to service. Instead, we first need to encourage faith and hope so that faith will become the wellspring of good works and love.

Article XXVI of *The Augsburg Confession* claims ". . .the Gospel demands that the teaching about faith should and must be emphasized in the church. . . "[1] Article XXVII says that ". . .righteousness of faith. . .should be emphasized above all else in the Christian church."[2]

I remember talking to one colleague a decade ago who argued that telling people they needed to have faith would give them the wrong impression, implying that they had to do something (believe) to be saved/justified. Consequently, this pastor made baptism and the covenant established there as one of the major themes of almost every sermon. He wanted to hammer home to the congregation that God is the only actor in salvation. On the other hand, he rarely mentioned faith and never insinuated that one had to possess it. I never did understand how this pastor explained the Apostle's call for people to "repent" or "believe" in the book of Acts.

I told this pastor that the difficulty with this emphasis on baptism is that both the Scriptures and the Lutheran confessions make it clear that without faith, it is impossible to please God. Without faith the sacrament is not beneficial. The XIII article of *The Apology of the Augsburg Confessions* states it is wrong:

> *...to believe that we are justified by a ceremony [sacraments] without a good disposition in our heart, that is, without faith. Yet this ungodly and wicked notion is taught with great authority throughout the papal realm. . .we teach that in using the sacraments there must be a faith which believes the promises and accepts that which is promised and offered in the sacrament. A promise is useless unless faith accepts it. The sacraments are signs of the promises. When they are used, therefore, there must be faith. . .*[3]

A couple of paragraphs later, Augustine is quoted: ". . .faith in the sacrament, and not the sacrament, justifies."[4] Immediately following is a reference to Romans 10:10, which states: "For it is with your heart that you believe and are justified."

Quotes like these would leave my colleague unmoved. He and others continue to speak of the benefits of baptism (forgiveness, eternal life, reconciliation with God) remaining intact in an adult, whether or not he has faith in Jesus Christ.

This neglect of faith has encouraged many clergy to cling to a baptismal universalism; that is, that once a person is baptized, she is saved forever, even if as an adult she has no faith. I was recently talking with a Lutheran pastor who admitted that he emphasized baptism while refusing to tell his flock that faith was necessary now that they were adults. I asked him if he believed that infant baptism saves a person when they are adults.

He answered, "Yes."

I then asked, "If an adult, who had been baptized as an infant, at present does not believe in God, despises Jesus Christ and deliberately lives an immoral life, do you think he is saved?"

My colleague replied, "Yes."

This belief in "once baptized, always saved" is unfortunately not limited to a few individual pastors. I have met many clergy who hold tenaciously to this theological conclusion. In the process, they nearly always think that they are defending confessional Lutheranism and preserving the doctrine of salvation by grace alone.

The dire consequence of this misunderstanding of Lutheran doctrine is the conclusion by these pastors that all members of the congregation they serve are in relationship with God simply because of baptism. The result is that the congregation continues to be told wholesale that they are God's children and in His family. They are asked to remember their baptisms and what God did for them there. This is all appropriate if addressed to people who have faith in Jesus Christ. However, those without faith (or the unrepentant) are being hypnotized with such talk into thinking that everything is well with their souls. This is a gross mistake because we give people without faith the false assurance that faith is not necessary. We then become an obstacle to people coming to a justifying faith because the Spirit has little with which to convict sinners.

Lutheran doctrine does not claim that baptized adults are saved or justified just because they are baptized. The definition of the church from the seventh article of *The Augsburg Confession* is ". . .the assembly of all *believers* among whom the Gospel is preached in its purity and the holy sacraments are administered according to the Gospel."[5] (Italics added). In article IV on Justification in *The Apology of the Augsburg Confession*, the article upon which we, as Lutherans, say the church stands or falls, the word faith appears four hundred times! In comparison, baptism appears only a few times, almost parenthetically. Yet, in many churches today, these have been flip-flopped. Our Lutheran forefathers communicated these words to adults who were all baptized. What was then necessary to complement that life-giving ceremony was a faith which through repentance renewed those baptismal waters and made them beneficial again and again.

Neither does Lutheran doctrine claim that baptized adults are unable to lose their salvation. In fact, it clearly teaches the opposite. The twelfth article of *The Augsburg Confession* rejects the teaching that ". . .persons who have once become godly cannot fall again."[6] Luther, in his *Large Catechism*, claims ". . .it does happen that we slip and fall out of the ship."[7] A couple paragraphs earlier we read: ". . .Baptism remains forever. Even though we fall from it and sin, nevertheless we always have access to it so that we may again subdue the old man."[8] It is my opinion that many pastors become confused with statements like "baptism remains forever." Phrases like these are often taken to mean that baptism is forever effectual for the recipient. That is not what the confessions say. They state that one can fall away from his baptism, and the old Adam can strangle him to death spiritually. However, the benefits of baptism remain accessible always, ready to be renewed by returning to it through a faith which repents.

The Treatise on the Power and Primacy of the Pope claims: ". . .countless souls are lost generation after generation…the true teaching must be embraced for the glory of God and the salvation of souls."[9] This reference to lost souls does not refer to those people who were not baptized, but instead to the baptized who do not have faith. It also mentions that the salvation of souls depends on embracing true teaching. When the church distorts the true teaching that faith needs to accompany baptism in the adult, then souls are lost.

The Apology of the Augsburg Confession states: "Faith does not remain in those who lose the Holy Spirit and reject penitence. . ."[10] The same article says: ". . .those who have fallen after Baptism can obtain the forgiveness of sins whenever, and as often as, they are converted."[11] Article VI states: "We say that eternal life is promised to the justified, but those who walk according to the flesh can retain neither faith nor righteousness."[12] The same article also claims: "Whoever casts away love will not keep his faith, be it ever so great, because he will not keep the Holy Spirit."[13]

The Solid Declaration says the ". . .Holy Scripture also assures us that God who has called us will be so faithful that after he has 'begun the good work in us' he will also continue it to the end and complete it, *if* we ourselves do not turn away from him. . ."[14] (Italics added). Article VII of the same work says that ". . .the Gospel is and remains the true Gospel even when godless hearers do not believe it (except that in them it does not effect salvation). . ."[15] Article IV also states:

> *. . .we must begin by earnestly criticizing and rejecting the false Epicurean delusion which some dream up that it is impossible to lose faith and the gift of righteousness and salvation. . .[also rejected is the thought] that even though a Christian follows his evil lusts without fear and shame, resists the Holy Spirit, and deliberately proceeds to sin against his conscience, he can nevertheless retain faith, the grace of God, righteousness, and salvation.*[16]

In the fourth article of *The Solid Declaration*, two Scriptures are quoted from the New Testament confirming the need for a person to have faith. The first is Matthew 24:13: ". . .only he who endures to the end will be saved. . ."[17] The second is Hebrews 3:14: "We share in Christ only if we hold our first confidence firm to the end."[18]

The second article of *The Solid Declaration* states:

> *If a person will not hear preaching or read the Word of God, but despises the Word and the community of God, dies in this condition, and perishes in his sins, he can neither comfort himself with God's eternal election nor obtain his mercy. . . [that person will] remain in the darkness of his unbelief and be lost. . .*[19]

Many passages in *The Book of Concord* repeat the belief that faith is necessary for salvation:

> *...faith makes the difference between those who are saved and those who are not...eternal life is promised to the justified and it is faith that justifies.*[20]
>
> *Faith takes hold of grace.*[21]
>
> *When frightened consciences are consoled by faith and believe that our sins are blotted out by Christ's death...then indeed Christ's suffering benefits us.*[22]

An all too prevalent opinion among my colleagues is the notion that a sacrament bestows benefits upon the recipient even if faith is not present. I asked the pastor who said that he believes that baptism saves even the adult who does not believe in God, despises Jesus Christ and deliberately lives an immoral life if he thought that was what Luther believed. He answered, "Yes." Many more clergy think the same way. It is as if God's saving grace is best shown when He gives relationship to people who do not know it or particularly desire it. Lutheran theology emphatically rejects this idea.

This misunderstanding about the sacraments has caused many to avoid talk of faith because it might minimize the holy sacrament. Many clergy baptize children of parents who show no signs of interest in faith or the church simply because they think that the ceremony of baptism grants salvation, regardless of the parent's interest in the spiritual training of the child. Communion is distributed to people indiscriminately, to the penitent and the non-penitent, as if God forgives people through the bread and wine, regardless of the presence or absence of faith and a repentant heart. Absolution is often given to everyone present as if that Word proclaimed from the pastor will give forgiveness to those who do not want it, seek it or desire an amendment of life.

I often debate baptismal practices with colleagues. I am shocked at how often I learn that many of them baptize children of unbelieving parents because they believe that baptism secures eternal life for the infant and connection with God indefinitely. Yet, the confessions state: "Where faith is present with its fruits there Baptism is no empty symbol...but where faith is lacking, it remains a mere unfruitful sign..."[23]

I have heard several pastors quote the following phrase from Luther's *Large Catechism* in an attempt to argue that baptism saves a soul and does not need a corresponding faith in an adult:

> *To appreciate and use Baptism aright, we must draw strength and comfort from it when our sins or conscience oppress us, and we must retort, "But I am baptized. . .I have the promise that I shall be saved and have eternal life, both in soul and body."*[24]

What pastors often neglect to mention is that to retort "I am baptized" in such a way is in itself a declaration of faith. It is only those of faith who can claim the benefits of baptism. This is confirmed by passages immediately before the above one. A few paragraphs earlier Luther proclaims:

> *. . .faith alone makes the person worthy to receive the salutary, divine water profitably. Since these blessings are offered and promised in the words which accompany the water, they cannot be received unless we believe them whole-heartedly. Without faith Baptism is of no use, although in itself it is an infinite, divine treasure.*[25]

The next paragraph continues this thought:

> *Just by allowing the water to be poured over you, you do not receive Baptism in such a manner that it does you any good. But it becomes beneficial to you if you accept it as God's command and ordinance, so that, baptized in the name of God, you may receive in the water the promised salvation. This the hand cannot do, nor the body, but the heart must believe it.*[26]

Clergy often miss the distinction that the sacrament is valid and active for all who receive it, but is not beneficial if there is no faith. It might be similar to having a social security card. A social security number is automatically issued to United States citizens when they are born. That number offers many benefits to the card holder: retirement money, disability, etc. Destroying the card does not disqualify the individual from the right to the benefits. The cardholder will always have access to them, even if the social security benefits, like disability or Medicare, are never used. Even though the person may never take advantage of what is freely offered, the offer still stands.

Attitudes concerning communion are sometimes similar. That is, many pastors hold to the false notion that communion imparts forgiveness and thus eternal life to all who receive it, regardless of their disposition toward God or acknowledgment of (or sorrow over) their sin. The confessions, however, consistently declare that faith needs to be present for the sacraments to be beneficial. The seventh article of *The Epitome* states:

> *...unbelievers receive the true body and blood of Christ; but if they are not converted and do not repent, they receive them not to life and salvation but to their judgment and condemnation... [Christ] is just as much present to exercise and manifest his judgment on unrepentant guests as he is to work life and consolation in the hearts of believing and worthy guests. We believe, teach, and confess that there is only one kind of unworthy guest, namely, those who do not believe.*[27]

In the *Large Catechism*, Luther states: . . .those who despise the sacrament and lead unchristian lives receive it to their harm and damnation."[28] We have often glorified the sacrament so that it now no longer needs faith as the confessors originally demanded. When we speak only of the sacrament and God's work through it, and completely ignore the faith of the recipient, we distort the truth. Failure to distinguish salvation's two parts, baptism and faith, has caused us to neglect communicating the necessary demands of the Gospel to the people with whom we minister. It has also often been an obstacle for people under our spiritual care to experience salvation.

It is clear to me that this hiding of the need for faith comes instinctively from the Lutheran desire to, above all else, protect the doctrine that humans lack free will in spiritual matters and the notion that God is the sole actor in salvation. *The Solid Declaration* states:

> *We believe that in spiritual and divine things the intellect, heart, and will of unregenerated man cannot by any native*

or natural powers in any way understand, believe, accept, imagine, will, begin, accomplish, do, effect, or cooperate, but that man is entirely and completely dead and corrupted as far as anything good is concerned. Accordingly, we believe that after the Fall and prior to his conversion not a spark of spiritual powers has remained or exists in man by which he could make himself ready for the grace of God . . .nor that he has any capacity for grace by and for himself or can apply himself to it or prepare himself for it, or help, do, effect, or cooperate toward his conversion by his own powers, either altogether or half-way or in the tiniest or smallest degree. . .[29]

Faith is a threat to the above doctrine when it is perceived as the fruit of human will or decision. Many Lutheran clergy have allowed a contemporary evangelical definition of faith to control their own definition. We avoid talk of faith because it has the connotation of a human act only because our American Christian ethos is permeated with a sense that faith is something we do, create or conjure up on our own. And so we abandon the ship "idea of faith" and leave it to float, listing and helpless, ready to sink at any moment. Then we jump into the life raft of "sacramentalism," devoid of faith, as if to protect God's sovereignty.

What is needed is to regain the use of both the term and the concept of "faith" by redeeming it from popular definition and resurrecting it with a confessional garb. First of all, we adamantly declare that faith does not have its source in human decision or will or emotion. It is foremost a gift of God. God gives us the ability to believe.

Imagine someone starving to death in the desert, unable to attain provision of any kind. Suddenly, he chances upon a huge fire pit with food cooking on a grill in its center. It is impossible for him to get at the food by himself. The fire is too hot, and the distance is too great. He would burn his hand before reaching the meat. Then he notices a very long pair of metal tongs lying nearby. Using the tongs, he is able to reach through the fire to grab the food from the grill. The tongs are not a part of him. They are a gift from whomever left them. They are the instrument by which he is able to receive the food he needs for survival.

In the same way, we cannot obtain the promise of eternal life of our own volition or with our own power. In fact, we are unaware of our spiritual hunger for those things before regeneration. We cannot take hold of the promise of life through Christ's suffering on our own. Instead, faith is given to us when the Spirit convinces us of our hunger, becoming the instrument by which we receive the promises of God for salvation. The confessions state again and again that it is faith that grasps the Gospel promise, and that faith is given as a gift from God:

> . . .*faith's sole office and property is to serve as the only and exclusive means and instrument with and through which we receive, grasp, accept, apply to ourselves, and appropriate the grace and the merit of Christ in the promise of the Gospel.*[30]

A good way to re-imagine faith, wresting it from its present false definitions and misunderstandings, is to renew the confessional image of spiritual blindness as the human condition before the Spirit works faith in an individual. Faith then becomes not an active part for us to play but simply the gift of sight, a spiritual healing performed by God. To have faith is to finally see ourselves and God clearly. We realize that we are sinners and that God offers new life in Christ because of His work on the cross and His resurrection. We see our sin and God's penalty for it, and then His wonderful grace brings about repentance. Because we can grow blind again to our sin and God's mercy, we continually need to hear the Word and to participate in the community of faith so that the Spirit continues to work faith (sight).

This image of blindness retains the need for faith in order to "see" oneself (sin) and God (His grace) clearly, and thus produce repentance and salvation (constant accessing of the waters of baptism). At the same time the image avoids any suggestion of human activity in the process. The idea of a blind person being healed cannot be construed as a result of human will or action. Faith is not a human decision to receive God's promises, but instead it is a clear vision (understanding) of God and self obtained by the miraculous healing of spiritual eyes.

The Scriptures often use the image of blindness to describe the human condition, as well as stating that God is the One who can open eyes to spiritual truth. In II Corinthians, Paul declares that "the god of this world has blinded the minds of the unbelievers, so that they cannot see the light of the gospel of the glory of Christ" (4:4). In II Corinthians 3:14-16 and 18, Paul declares:

> ...to this day, the same veil remains when the old covenant is read. The veil has not been removed, because only in Christ is it taken away. Even to this day when Moses is read, a veil covers their hearts. But whenever anyone turns to the Lord, the veil is taken away. . .And we, who with unveiled faces all reflect the Lord's glory, are being transformed into his likeness with ever-increasing glory which comes from the Lord, who is the Spirit.

What Paul is describing here is faith, the gift of seeing self and God which "comes from the Lord."

In Acts 26:18 Paul claims that God sent him to the Gentiles "...to open their eyes, and turn from darkness to light, and from the power of Satan to God, so that they may receive forgiveness of sins...by faith in me." Acts 16:14 describes Lydia's coming to faith: "The Lord opened her heart to respond to Paul's message." This describes faith passively. It is another way of saying that the Lord gave Lydia eyes to see Him.

On the road to Emmaus in Luke twenty-four, the resurrected Jesus joins Cleopas and his friend on their journey. Although Jesus joins them, the Scriptures state that "[their eyes] were kept from recognizing him" (Luke 24:16). The method Jesus used to open their eyes was to quote Scripture to them. As he did so, their hearts burned within them. The two travelers invited Jesus to stay with them that evening, and at the meal Jesus blessed the bread, broke it, and gave it to them. The sentence Luke uses to describe that event is the identical sentence he uses at the narrative of the Last Supper when Jesus handled the bread for communion. In the twenty-fourth chapter of Luke, the bread is used for a regular meal, but the allusion to the Last Supper is intended. As a result of their encounter with the Word and the sacrament, ". . .their eyes were opened and they recognized him. . ." (Luke 24:31).

The road to Emmaus story is a paradigm of an individual coming to faith in Jesus Christ. Every human being's spiritual eyes are kept from recognizing God, sin, or a need for a Savior. It is only through an encounter with the Word and sacrament, however, that the Holy Spirit opens human eyes so that hearts can see their sin, know God, and trust Jesus for forgiveness and life.

In his Gospel, John seems to use "seeing" and "believing" interchangeably. In the first part of the ninth chapter, John portrays Jesus as healing a man of his physical blindness. At the end of the chapter, through His words, Jesus heals the man's spiritual blindness and guides him to a faith in the Messiah. Here, seeing means believing. Then Jesus tells the man: "...for judgment I have come into this world, that the blind will see and those who see will become blind" (John 9:39).

In John 20:8, when the disciple John enters the empty tomb where only the linens that covered Jesus' body remained, we read that John "saw and believed" even though he did not actually see anything physical. John, the author, has Mary Magdalene walking to the tomb in the dark, in stark contrast to the other three Gospels where it was dawn. John is communicating something spiritual, not chronological. Throughout his Gospel John often uses the metaphor of light when talking about relationship with God. Mary was in the dark that first Easter morning because she did not know that Jesus was alive. In the garden, Jesus encounters Mary. She does not recognize Him until He calls her by name. When she later related this experience to the disciples she simply said, "I have seen the Lord!" John thinks of faith as the ability to know and see God even when one sees nothing material.

The Formula of Concord often uses the image of blindness to describe the spiritual condition of humans before God works faith in them:

> *. . .in spiritual matters man's understanding and reason are **blind** and that he understands nothing by his own powers. . .*[31]

> *. . .man is so corrupted that in divine things, concerning our conversion and salvation, he is by nature **blind** and does not and cannot understand the Word of God when it is preached, but considers it foolishness; nor does he of himself approach God, but he is and remains an enemy of God until by the power of the Holy Spirit, through the Word which is preached and heard, purely out of grace and without any cooperation on his part, he is converted, becomes a believer, is regenerated and renewed.*[32]

> . . .although man's reason or natural intellect still has a dim spark of the knowledge that there is a God. . .nevertheless, it is so ignorant, **blind**, and perverse that even when the most gifted and the most educated people on earth read or hear the Gospel of the Son of God and promise of eternal salvation, they cannot by their own powers perceive this, comprehend it, understand it, or believe and accept it as the truth.[33]

> Luther. . .states that **blind** and captive man performs only the devil's will and what is contrary to the Lord God. . .God himself must draw man and give him new birth.[34]

> . . .the Lord God draws the person whom he wills to convert, and draws him in such a way that man's darkened reason becomes an enlightened one and his resisting will becomes an obedient will.[35]

We must no longer exalt baptism at the expense of faith in order to protect God's sovereign work in salvation or because pastors of some denominations define faith poorly. Instead, we need to identify baptism as a great treasure and gift in which God brings us single-handedly into His family, while also adamantly declaring that only by faith can we honor that ceremony and participate in its benefits. The image of faith being the sight God gives humans to see their sin and His provision in Christ helps preserve this need for faith, without threatening the doctrine of no free will in the saving process.

We also need a solid new image for what baptism is and what it accomplishes. A wrong understanding of it is commonplace. Baptism is viewed by some clergy as a kind of spiritual cure-all, a magic wand which once waved over a baby seals and permanently secures that individual's connection with God.

An image I would like to propose for infant baptism, which might serve as a corrective to many present errors, is one of betrothal. But for it to be appropriate, it needs to be a betrothal that is established by the parents before the child is capable of making a personal decision, a practice that still exists in parts of the world.

In Shakespeare's play, *Romeo and Juliet*, the culture in which the drama took place was one where parents selected a mate for their daughter while she was very young and unable to make good decisions of this kind on her own. Juliet was most likely in her early teens when her parents betrothed her to a certain man whom they no doubt thought would be a good husband for her. Juliet was not involved in the decision.

Apparently, the contract of betrothal established between Juliet's father and the husband-to-be was binding regardless of Juliet's attitude toward it. She could not escape the contract, except through death (which she tried to fake after she had fallen for Romeo). She did not desire to wed the man her parents had selected. She had decided that she would not affirm her betrothal by saying, "I do" at her wedding. Even though she had a contractual relationship with one man, she loved another with her heart.

Juliet could not tell her parents that she did not want to marry their choice for her. She was not in a position to decline the marriage. So she faked her death on the night before her scheduled wedding. Because Romeo had failed to learn of her plan, he was convinced she actually had died. He found her body in the vault and killed himself before she awoke from the potion that the friar had given her. When she saw her dead lover, Juliet then killed herself.

In baptism, our parents betroth us to Jesus Christ. It is a binding covenant despite the infant's lack of involvement in the decision process. While we may find the process of parents choosing a marriage partner for their young child unacceptable, there is only one Person who would be the right spiritual partner for any child: Jesus Christ. So the parents establish a covenant of betrothal between their child and God at baptism, hoping and praying that one day that child will say, "I do" and commit her whole life to Him (what confirmation theoretically is supposed to be).

The only way to get out of the baptismal covenant of betrothal is to die. As the baptized child grows into adulthood, if he becomes infatuated by another god and gives himself to it, he will die spiritually and thus lose the benefits of baptism. Yet, the waters of baptism are ever close, and the life they bestow can easily be taken up again as a person returns to them through repentance.

This image retains the binding nature of baptism while demanding daily affirmation of that betrothal as an adult. It also acknowledges that one can be severed from relationship with God and lose the benefits of baptism.

In the *Small Catechism*, Luther states: ". . .on the last day [God] will raise me and all the dead and will grant eternal life to me and to all who believe in Christ."[36] Salvation demands faith as well as baptism. Yet, the church often neglects faith in our preoccupation with baptism. As a result we are guilty of keeping vital information concerning salvation from the people we pastor.

Mark 16:16 states "Whoever believes and is baptized will be saved. . ." Often, however, we forget the rest of the verse: ". . .but whoever does not believe will be condemned." The second half leaves out reference to baptism, insinuating that one can be baptized and not be saved. It is imperative that we confirm the Scripture's and the *Confession's* declaration that faith is an essential part of salvation. We need to make faith an integral topic of our preaching and teaching. We should pray for those in our congregation who do not have a living faith in Jesus Christ that the Holy Spirit would work faith in them through the congregation's teaching and preaching. If we emphasize baptism and neglect a regular call to faith, we will create a religious people who have no real or vibrant connection with Jesus Christ. If we do claim faith's necessity, however, we will help bring a renewal to our denomination.

DISTINCTION 2

General and Saving Grace

The failure of so many Lutheran pastors to distinguish between a common grace, whereby God showers the blessings of physical life on all people regardless of their disposition toward Him, and a grace that justifies the sinner and brings spiritual life to people only through the special means of Word and sacrament, has caused grave consequences for the life of the church. When common grace is seen as the sole way in which God communicates life to the human race, one quickly moves toward a doctrine of universal salvation in which all people are in a saving relationship with God automatically, regardless of faith or repentance, just because God loves and accepts all people unconditionally. I admit that I myself prefer this option and would welcome the salvation of all souls, not only those who trust in Jesus Christ. However, the Scriptures and the Lutheran confessions make it clear that salvation (renewed relationship with God) is only mediated through the Word and sacraments and is received by faith. Without those means, a person is unable to receive the justifying grace of God.

I have been surprised at how many Lutheran clergy in the past decades have abandoned such a basic concept as salvation by faith through Christ alone. Whenever I converse with clergy who have the notion that all people are saved, even without repentance and faith, I am struck with their sincere love for humanity. I appreciate their disdain for those who call for a strict adherence to the belief that those who do not have faith like ours are eternally separated from God, and then often seem to be more interested in right doctrine than in the lives of those who would perish under such a rule. No doubt many who are universalists are pushed further in their convictions when they encounter others who they think are determined to make sure that unbelievers "get what's coming to them" by ending up in hell.

Regardless of our own desires or opinions on the matter, the fact remains that the Scriptures and the confessions speak about God's grace, given so that sinners might be reconciled and received by faith through the means of Word and sacrament. This truth makes it imperative that the church provide the Word and sacraments in such a way that non-believers might be inspired to a saving faith. One of the grave consequences of universalism is that one loses a sense of urgency to proclaim the Gospel to unbelievers and to support missionary endeavors, something that has always been the central, unique work of the church.

The difficult and almost impossible obstacles for many Lutheran clergy are the notions of hell, God's wrath and the eternal separation of unbelievers. These concepts seem so incompatible with God's mercy, patience and unconditional love for sinners. Holding both thoughts simultaneously—that of a loving God, and this same God allowing the eternal destruction of all who do not believe in Jesus—seems impossible. This is exacerbated by Luther and Calvin's beliefs that humans have no free will in spiritual matters, that all humanity is blind to their own sin, and that we are unable to fear, love and trust God or make a decision for Him apart from the Word and Spirit. How can those who cannot come to know God on their own, without His help, be held responsible for their failure to believe in a Savior they cannot choose? How could God condemn them to hell, especially when we know He loves all people so deeply?

Since the Enlightenment, when rationalism gained more ground, the doctrines of judgment and hell have been a major stumbling block for many Christians seeking to ignore those uncomfortable doctrines, and instead emphasizing only God's mercy and grace. The thought of God's wrath and eternal hell for non-believers has been a major reason why many thoughtful theists in the past three centuries have found a home in Deism, in Unitarianism, or simply in personal reverence for God expressed outside of any community of faith rather than in Christianity.

But the fact remains that Protestant theology distinguishes between a "common" or "general" grace and a "justifying" or "saving" grace. Each is mediated differently: the former indiscriminately on all people for their general welfare, and the latter only on those who encounter it through the Word and sacraments and receive it by faith.

Luther spoke about the general grace of God that He showers upon all people, no matter what their theological beliefs or moral integrity. God provides physical life to all people through employment, food, family and government. Even though people turn their backs on God, He still graciously loves and provides for them.

Psalm 136:25 claims that God "...gives food to every creature. His love endures forever." In Matthew 5:45 Jesus states that the Father in heaven "...causes His sun to rise on the evil and the good, and sends rain on the righteous and the unrighteous." That this is an awesome gesture of grace by the perfect God to imperfect and undeserving humans is beyond dispute.

In Genesis, genealogies appear after the sins of Cain, after the story of universal wickedness at the time of the flood and after the tower of Babel incident. Many scholars see this placement as a deliberate attempt to display God's grace. Humans quit serving and worshipping God, but God keeps human life going. The genealogies attest to the fact that the God who gives life has not quit sustaining it for sinful people.

When Paul is speaking to the non-believers at Lystra, he tells them that God "...has shown kindness by giving you rain from heaven and crops in their seasons; he provides you with plenty of food and fills your hearts with joy" (Acts 14:17). The Scriptures teach that God loves all people and that His giving of all things necessary for life and joy is an unconditional act. God does not abandon the wicked, but instead constantly helps them and provides for them.

Yet, it is essential for us to understand that this grace that provides for physical life does not return sinners to God's family. This is not the grace that justifies sinners and brings salvation. Justifying grace comes to fallen sinners through means ordained by God. Furthermore, that grace is administered only through those means, and an individual needs to receive this grace by faith.

Article V of *The Augsburg Confession* states:

> *To obtain such faith God instituted the office of the ministry, that is, provided the Gospel and the sacraments. Through these, as through means, he gives the Holy Spirit, who works faith, when and where he pleases, in those who hear the Gospel.*[37]

The key to justification is faith. Faith receives the grace that justifies. Faith is a work of the Holy Spirit in an individual enabling him to understand this great gift and to receive it. The Holy Spirit does not work this faith directly from heaven but instead only through the means of Word and sacrament. That is why the office of the ministry has been instituted.

In other words, God's saving grace is offered to spiritually blind and deaf humans as the Word is proclaimed and the sacraments are received. Unfortunately, no human has eyes or heart enough to see or acknowledge that grace, let alone his need for it, until the Holy Spirit creates faith in that person—a faith that acknowledges both his need for that grace and God's provision of it through Christ. Without the Word and sacrament, the Holy Spirit cannot create faith in a human heart, and without the Holy Spirit no human heart can believe and accept that grace.

I was on a pastoral retreat a number of years ago, staying in a cabin on a Minnesota lake. During some free time, I decided to run around the lake, a journey I estimated to be just a few miles at the most, a distance I could handle. But when I had completed what I thought must have been three miles, I discovered that I was only halfway around the lake. I knew that six miles would be too much for me.

I continued to run, becoming increasingly tired. I also became aware of a growing thirst. I had brought no water along, and I began to dream of getting a glassful when I got back to the cabin. To make matters worse, with a couple miles still left to go, it began to rain. This gave me added incentive to keep on running.

I was hot and sore and extremely thirsty. I looked at the rain falling all around me and thought it a cruel joke that all the water I needed surrounded me, but I could not receive enough of it into my body to relieve my deep thirst.

The rain was falling on the fields of corn and beans on either side of the road, and I became jealous of those plants that were benefiting from the moisture I could not obtain. The rain would eventually benefit me and all people in the area by providing the food we needed, but that water could not quench my immediate thirst.

I knew where to go to quench my thirst. The problem was that I was still a long way from it. Eventually, I stumbled back to the cabin, exhausted. I immediately went inside to find the water which I was so desperately seeking. I entered the kitchen, went straight to the sink, turned on the faucet, grabbed a glass, filled it and drank the cold, refreshing water. That water, although similar to the stuff falling from the sky outside, satisfied my need in a way the rain could not.

This illustration might be helpful as we seek to distinguish between general grace and justifying grace. General grace is like the rain that falls on all things indiscriminately. Nothing exposed escapes it. Saving grace is like the water that comes from a particular faucet, giving people the moisture needed to survive.

The faucet is connected to pipes which go deep into the well far below the surface. It is like the Word and sacrament, the elements that make available the water needed for human spiritual life. The cabinet in which the faucet is installed is like the church that props up that "faucet" in such a way that others have access to it. The water far below the surface is unattainable to an individual. It is hidden far beneath rock and earth. Well-drillers must drill through those obstacles in order to make the valuable water available. Similarly, the grace that justifies is inaccessible to us. Christ Jesus "drilled" a hole through the obstacles of unbelief and sin, making God's grace accessible to spiritually thirsty people.

But even if the well is dug, the pipes set in the right place, and the faucet installed in the vanity, the Water is still not accessible without a pumpand without turning on the faucet. This compares to the process of salvation: even though Jesus Christ died and rose again (making an opening between God and humans), and even though the church makes the Word and sacrament available to the world, saving grace cannot and will not be accessed without the Holy Spirit (the power that makes the connection between God and man possible). The Holy Spirit is also the One who calls and moves individuals toward the "faucets" of Word and sacrament that the church makes available. The Spirit works the faith in people and brings them forward to receive the water from the faucet. The faith that the Spirit creates receives the grace that justifies.

Once we make the distinction between common grace and justifying grace, it is possible to halt our widespread retreat from evangelism and start an aggressive counter-attack. When we understand that even though all people are unconditionally loved by God but lost and separated from spiritual life without faith, then we gain new energy and incentive to share the Word of God and proclaim the risen Lord. We suddenly realize that our efforts to share Christ through the Word are of utmost importance, and the Word is indeed calling us to act in this regard.

Whenever I hear my colleagues espouse universal salvation and show a corresponding lack of interest in evangelism, I cannot help but marvel at how their attitude denies the office of the ministry. Universalism rejects the belief that faith is necessary for salvation; that evangelism is a life-and-death enterprise; that the Word and sacrament are necessary means for a dead person to come alive to God; and that the Holy Spirit in a person is what quickens that dead life. When talking recently to a respected colleague, she said that she believes that all people are in relationship to God automatically because Jesus died, and that being a Christian is not necessary, nor for that matter is having a belief in God. It is just a perk. When she made these claims, I was struck at how much Biblical, traditional and confessional Christianity was thrown out the window at those sweeping claims. Particularly, the need for evangelism melts away. Universalism steps on all the toes of Lutheran confessionalism, Biblical claims and the practice of Christianity for two thousand years. To hold to Universalism is to deny the authority of the Scriptures and the confessions.

Article IV of *The Augsburg Confession* states the necessity of an individual's faith in salvation:

> . . .*we receive forgiveness of sin and become righteous before God by grace, for Christ's sake, through faith, when we believe that Christ suffered for us and that for his sake our sin is forgiven and righteousness and eternal life are given to us.*[38]

Lutheran theology states unequivocally that a person needs to have faith to be in a saving relationship with God. Of course, we understand that faith is a creation and gift of God to one who is otherwise dead, blind and unable either to know God or to move toward Him. Regardless of its source or origin, or of the dynamics of its creation, an adult absolutely needs to have faith in Jesus Christ to receive forgiveness and eternal life.

So, then, faith is necessary. But for faith to be created, the Holy Spirit's work is necessary. For the Holy Spirit to operate, the Word and sacraments need to be available. For the Word and sacraments to be available, the church needs to deliver it. We, the church, are essential elements in the process of individuals coming to a justifying faith and thus to reconciliation with God.

One good way to restore a healthy interest in evangelism and in preaching that encourages faith is to renew an interest in and commitment to the Lutheran confessions. On the other hand, continued failure to share the Word for the purpose of faith creation, and thus salvation, is a blatant denial of both Scripture and the confessions. To be Biblical, to be confessional, is to believe that without the Word, people die. And we are the only ones who have it in our possession to share.

A clear distinction between common/general grace and justifying grace is then essential for the church and its pastors. It is this failure to distinguish between these two kinds of grace that has decimated evangelism. It has generated a universalism that is neither Biblical nor Lutheran. It has caused many pastors to share God's love without warning unbelievers that in spite of that love, they are separated from a justifying relationship with God. We have often failed to call others to a faith that justifies by itself. If we do not regain a proper understanding and conviction of this distinction, we will fail at the Great Commission to which Jesus has called us. If we can regain it, we might be able to proclaim Jesus Christ to the world with new energy and conviction. It is in His name alone we find life with God.

DISTINCTION 3

The Word: Law and Gospel

In discussions with other clergy on general preaching philosophies, time and again I have heard the phrase, "I would rather err on the side of the Gospel," meaning in contrast to the law. The problem with paradoxes and distinctions, however, is that erring in regard to putting too much emphasis on either is equally disastrous. One might as well say, "I would rather have the engine of the car than the body and wheels." A strong focus on the Gospel at the expense of the law has been a general tendency in the preaching of our denomination. Consequently, our preaching has often been hollow and ineffective.

The common criticism from evangelicals that mainline denominations do not "preach the Gospel" is really a criticism that they do not preach the law. I have to agree that in many quarters of the ELCA the law/Gospel dialectic has been virtually abandoned for a Gospel-only theology. The "Word" is often defined unconsciously as the Gospel instead of law/Gospel. The importance of distinguishing the Word into its two parts cannot be emphasized too much.

In Luther's time, four men were commissioned to visit Lutheran congregations to gain an understanding of current beliefs and practices among both pastors and laypeople. They were horrified at what they discovered. Pastors were getting drunk, and most had concubines. Many lay people had not received communion in over a year. There was great ignorance among the masses regarding basic Christian doctrine, and Biblical illiteracy was rampant. One of the great early Lutheran leaders, Philip Melencthon, suggested that the law be preached so as to rid the church of these evil practices. Another leader named Agricola wanted only the Gospel to be preached. He thought that the proclamation of God's graciousness would eventually be enough to turn people away from their evil practices. Luther intervened and stressed the need for both law and Gospel to be preached and taught. As a result of this debate, Luther wrote both the *Large Catechism* and the *Small Catechism*.

In his commentary on Psalm 90, Luther states that Moses ". . .performs the ministry of the Law; he depicts death in the most repulsive colors and in this way demonstrates that God's wrath is the cause of our death."[39] Later he says that in the Psalm Moses performs ". . .his special office of terrifying sinners."[40] Elsewhere in the same work Luther puts it bluntly, ". . .God is a God of wrath."[41] This kind of talk is often offensive to us. When I used the above quotes in a senior paper at seminary, one classmate was aghast and exclaimed, "I do not want a God like that!" Several others adamantly agreed. Unfortunately, we cannot pick and choose our theology based on how palatable or believable or comfortable it seems to us. We are committed both to the Bible and to the Lutheran confessions. We must give up our personal opinions as leaders of our faith and submit to the teachings that have withstood the test of time.

As difficult as it may be to say, we, like Moses in Psalm 90, are to be ministers ". . .of death, sin, and damnation."[42] The reason for this is not to be mean and insensitive. Instead, our aim should be ". . .to terrify the proud and to set squarely before the eyes of those who are smug in their sins their terrible condition, to cover up and to hide nothing."[43] Yet Lutherans often hide the law because it seems to contradict the notion of God's love and mercy. Several Lutheran pastors I know have the philosophy that if they only speak of God's love and mercy, then the Gospel will be embraced by the hearers. But the Scriptures and the confessions argue that the Gospel will not be received unless the law precedes it.

The law that drives one to Christ comes through means other than words and sermons. The law, in this function, is anything that reveals our true condition, which is separation from God and a nature that is curved in on itself. This is most clearly communicated to us through the reality of our death. In his Psalm 90 commentary, Luther states that the theme of the law: "In the midst of earthly life, snares of death surround us."[44] As we look at death and perceive that it is the fruit of our sin, we began to be able to hear the invitation of the Gospel: "In the midst of certain death, life in Christ is ours."[45]

The purpose of the law in this sense is simply to reveal reality to the human being. The reality of human life before faith is that we are enemies of God and cut off from relationship with Him. As a consequence of this sin, we are spiritually dead. We are lost. We are poor. We are doomed to separation from God forever. There is nothing we can do to change that.

The fear that we pastors have about the law is that it will be preached as "hellfire and brimstone"; that is, in such a way that the hearers are shamed and accused personally. If we think of the law as statements of reality, we do not have to share it in a manner that personally indicts every individual present. We can simply keep stating the general reality that humans without Christ are spiritually lost, separated from God and in need of salvation. We can relate that message in gentle, calm speech. Then we can trust the Holy Spirit to do the work of convicting hearts and convincing people of their sin. We do not need to know each individual's status with God. But we do need to clearly articulate the reality of human nature and the need for constant repentance before God.

The Gospel, on the other hand, invites lost people into a new reality. This news comes to those who, because of the law, know their sin and understand that they can do nothing to escape its consequences by their own efforts. This invitation to life and restoration of relationship with God comes through the person of Jesus Christ, who by His death and resurrection opened up this possibility. The Gospel invites us to faith in Jesus, upon whose coattails we ride into God's family.

As people trust in the work of Jesus on their behalf, they find themselves, by sheer grace, in a new reality: they are now children of God, spiritually alive, forgiven and fitted with an awesome destiny. Yet, after this new reality becomes ours, it is possible to lose it again. Every day we struggle to hold on to it by the grace of God. The old nature which clings to us seeks to lure us back to the old reality. Consequently, the law needs to continually be preached and heard, even by Christians, so that the sinful nature can drown daily through repentance.

The Gospel is an invitation to join God, given to one who is still in the old reality, and an invitation to remain with God for those who are already in God's family. It is not uncommon in Lutheran churches that the Gospel is made a general statement of reality instead of an invitation into a new reality. If this is the case, many people in the pews get the notion on Sunday mornings that they are spiritually healthy simply because Jesus died, and because they were baptized as an infant. The sense of urgency that the proclaimed Gospel needs to be received by faith every time it is heard is lost. It is a distortion of the Gospel to proclaim to adults that salvation was taken care of once and for all in infant baptism.

Imagine a strong and confident swimmer who is taking a swim in the ocean. He keeps his eye on the shore and continually monitors the distance back. He doesn't realize that strong currents will make it impossible for him to return on his own. Even the strongest swimmer in the world could not make it back. The Coast Guard, aware of the swimmer's plight, rushes out in a boat to save him. As they pull along side of the swimmer, somebody throws a life preserver out, and it lands within arm's length of the man.

"Grab the ring and we will save you," calls out a man on the boat.

"No, thanks, I'm fine," answers the swimmer as he continues confidently on his way.

The coast guard crew's first task is to convince the swimmer of the reality of his dangerous and hopeless situation. They must convince the swimmer that he will die if he doesn't accept their help. Only when the swimmer finally understands his plight will he hear the good news that the life preserver is there to save him. Only then will he desire to reach out and grab it.

People who do not understand their separation from God will have no interest in embracing the Gospel. If we simply "throw out" the Gospel and assume that because somebody hears it he will be saved from his sin, we will make a grave mistake. It is not enough to say, "Here's the Gospel, you are now in a new reality because of it." The church's first task is to convince the lost that they are drowning and in need of the help that only God can give. We first help them to understand the reality of their condition. This is the role of the law as we use it wisely and lovingly. When the hearer becomes convinced of his need for God, then the Gospel we share will be seized and clung to.

The Apology states: "All scripture should be divided into these two chief doctrines, the law and the promises."[46] Later it says, ". . .the law works wrath; it only accuses; it only terrifies consciences."[47] And again, ". . .the proclamation of rewards and punishments is necessary. In the proclamation of punishments the wrath of God is displayed, and hence this belongs to the preaching of penitence."[48]

The article on penitence in *The Apology* states:

> . . .it [is] *God's alien work to terrify because God's own proper work is to quicken and console. But he terrifies, he says, to make room for consolation and quickening because hearts that do not feel God's wrath in their smugness spurn consolation. In this way, Scripture makes a practice of joining these two, terror and consolation. . .*[49]

The Smalcald Articles say it this way:

> *[The law] is the thunderbolt by means of which God with one blow destroys both open sinners and false saints. He allows no one to justify himself. He drives all together into terror and despair. This is the hammer of which Jeremiah speaks, "is not my word like a hammer which breaks the rock in pieces?" (Jeremiah 23:29)*[50]

The Solid Declaration states:

> *. . .the Spirit of Christ must not only comfort but, through the office of the law, must also convince the world of sin. Thus, even in the New Testament, he must perform what the prophet calls 'a strange deed' (that is, to rebuke) until he comes to his own work (that is, to comfort and to preach about grace).*[51]

Later it states, ". . .Christ says 'the Holy Spirit will convince the world of sin' (John 16:8), which cannot be done without the explanation of the law."[52] Again:

> *. . .both doctrines are always together, and both of them have to be urged side by side, but in proper order and with the correct distinction. Therefore we justly condemn the Antinomians or nomoclasts who cast the preaching of the law out of the churches and would have us criticize sin and teach contrition and sorrow not from the law but solely from the Gospel.*[53]

One of my colleagues refuses to preach the law. His opinion is that if one hears the Gospel enough, she will eventually become captivated by God's great love for her and come to faith. This pastor's messages are centered on conveying the good news: ". . .God so loved the world that He gave his one and only Son. . ." (John 3:16). This pastor and others have rejected the Lutheran doctrine that the law needs to precede the Gospel if the Gospel is to be rightly received. When this doctrine is rejected, the Gospel's power to save sinners is greatly diminished.

The law is similar to having free salted peanuts or popcorn available in a bar. The goal of the owner is to sell liquor. Salted snacks are made available to all without charge to help increase the thirst of those eating them. Similarly, the law not only increases one's thirst for God, but in its initial stages helps one recognize that he has a spiritual thirst. Our goal is to deliver the "beverage" that quenches that human thirst. To accentuate that need/thirst, we make the law available to help one take notice of his need for the Living Water. Just as salt has been clearly shown to increase thirst, the church's employment of the law has made it clear that it increases a thirst for the Gospel.

Some clergy today are "Gospel only" preachers. They proceed, like my colleague above, with the opinion that the Gospel alone can accomplish salvation in an individual. However, the power of God to change lives, convert sinners and retain the saints is not accomplished through the Gospel alone. This happens as the Spirit works through the law and the Gospel together. I believe that we will have a difficult time converting sinners or bringing people into a lively relationship with God in our churches if we neglect the preaching of the law.

One obstacle for us clergy in embracing the law is the negative connotation we have of it. If the law is misused or handled poorly, it will turn people off to the Gospel. Maybe a better way to phrase it would be to say that the law can be couched in a manner that makes one doubt that the God described could possibly have grace and mercy as sweet as the Bible says.

We need to regain a healthy way to wield the sword of the law in such a manner that it does not kill the victim, but instead cuts away the veils before the eyes of the hearers so that they can see themselves clearly. We can be honest about the status of a life without God, without personally attacking or self-righteously condemning. The law simply makes statements about spiritual reality. It reveals the moral and spiritual failure of all humans. It does not need to single out certain individuals for special recognition. In this way, the preacher can sympathetically declare the sad state of an individual without God in general without needing to point the message at a particular person.

The former *Minneapolis Tribune* columnist Jim Klobuchar shared the power of the law in his life in leading him to repentance and an embrace of God's grace. But the law was not preached from the pulpit. He found it in a treatment center for addictions where he was sent by a court order. Klobuchar had previous experience with the church. He had heard sermons and had rubbed shoulders with Christians. But the Gospel never hit home until, for the first time in his life, the reality of his hopeless situation made him seek mercy from God.

Klobuchar shares his experience in his book *Pursued By Grace*. One day during his rehabilitation, he states:

> *I was seated in front of the blackboard in a semicircle with six other members of the group, all of them forced into treatment by court order, as I was. . .my chances depended entirely on how I read what I saw in white chalk whether I was serious or unconvinced about my alcoholism. . .on this afternoon, the white chalk on the blackboard had put me at a junction in my life where I probably would stand again. My instincts were prodding me with that warning and practically shouting it. Look hard and deep at what you see today, man, at this moment. Do you recognize yourself? Do you understand now the destruction you have caused? The bookkeeping was on the board, stark and inescapable, written in the counselor's hand but drawn from my own deposition. It was the first time I'd been exposed to a full accounting of thirty years of drinking. . .The last column was the one I dreaded. It told of the damage, first to personal honesty, because drinking led to infidelity and deceit. . .My daughters' lives were damaged. . . My marriages were damaged and the second one destroyed. The losses mounted. . .At the finish, the counselor was about to run out of board space. The final damage in the 1990s, at least as registered on the blackboard, was the second*

> *divorce, tens of thousands of dollars lost in the settlement and attorney's fees, a $700 fine on the DWI charge, two days in the workhouse, and thousands of dollars in added insurance premiums...Finally, the counselor said, "There's no category for the damage that you have done to yourself"...it was the only judgment, or implied judgment, he made. The rest was etched in chalk. I stared at it, overwhelmed.. The counselor stood at the blackboard, looking into my eyes, trying to be generous...he said, "What do you think?" I couldn't answer. ..What I believed first, at that moment, were the truths of the silent judgment on the blackboard. The truth was that I was an alcoholic...I said I had just looked into a mirror and it left me numb. It exposed the seamiest side of my life in a way that tolerated no denial. It showed me the truth as I had never pictured it and as I had refused to picture it.*[54]

Jim Klobuchar was confronted by the law. It did not come in religious terminology or from the pulpit, but it came. His moral failure was finally acknowledged. He was crushed, and despair swept over him as he realized that he could not wipe out the past or succeed in the future on his own. The law, as applied creatively by a wise counselor, helped Klobuchar clearly to see reality for the first time. It opened his eyes to his sin and failure. It also opened his heart to the Gospel where he heard of a God who embraces sinners.

Klobuchar could not continue the session. He excused himself and went to his room where he knelt by his bed, a broken man. He was too stricken to pray. Then he got up and went to the window where he could see a beautiful sunset. In that small room, Klobuchar experienced the grace of God in an invisible embrace. He, though being a failure and a sinner, was nevertheless accepted by the Creator. Klobuchar became a Christian.

Our churches are full of Klobuchars, men and women who attend services but have never experienced the grace of God. These people have not yet seen their moral failures, nor have they comprehended the consequences of being separated from God. If we only preach the Gospel to these needy people, they may never know or admit the reality of their sin. We do them a disservice by refusing to tell them the truth concerning their lives.

The law is not some nasty accusation of another. It is a mirror we seek to hold up in order that the other may see himself clearly and thus discover his need for God's grace and forgiveness. The human condition, besides being one of failure before God, is also one of a deep denial of one's failure. Only God the Spirit can open a person's spiritual eyes to see his sin. Only the Spirit can bring a soul to confession and repentance. Only the Spirit can overwhelm a person with the knowledge of God's marvelous grace.

But the Spirit cannot work this spiritual healing without our help. The Spirit does His work through the Word—both law and Gospel—as it is delivered by the church through circumstances and sometimes in surprising ways we could never imagine.

We pastors need to wisely administer the law in ways that resemble the counselor involved in Klobuchar's spiritual transformation. We should present it creatively, at appropriate times, with an overflow of compassion and prayer. We need simply to present it and stand back, trusting the Spirit to do the rest. We will be viewed by some (who are in denial of their terrible spiritual situation) as being wrong about our assessment, as Klobuchar viewed the counselor. Our words about sin and separation from God may be rejected. But those who disagree with us need to see that we harbor no personal judgments. They need to see our overwhelming love for them. The counselor did not hammer Klobuchar with his sins; he simply helped him to acknowledge their reality. The hammer came from within, through conscience and through the working of the Spirit. Our preaching, teaching and pastoral counseling can do the same.

Our refusal to use the law honestly and openly in our churches is like throwing a wet towel on the fire of the Gospel. If we do not revive an appropriate proclamation of the law, the Gospel will lose its power among us. If we continue to make the Gospel a statement of reality instead of a daily invitation to a new reality, we will create congregations that grow smug and cold, having little desire or need to embrace the Gospel as if their lives depended on it. Our sinfulness and God's grace need to stand together. Each self-destructs without the other. The Word we are called to present to a dying world needs to be couched with both law and Gospel. As we do that, the Word can work miracles.

DISTINCTION 4

Language: Technical and Psychological

There is an almost universal loathing for language of decision among ELCA Lutheran pastors. There is an unwritten list of "naughty" words and phrases that we pastors make sure we avoid, especially when conversing with each other. Among these banned words are "decide," "accept" and "conversion." Many often refuse to use "commitment to Christ," "come to Christ" or any language that suggests that a person can make any move or participate in any way in salvation. It is thought that such language compromises the theology that humans do nothing in salvation, and God does everything. These words, implying that people can act in the saving process, cloud the reality of human inability to fear, love and trust God, or to make any move whatsoever toward faith on their own. It is the noble objective of most of us Lutheran clergy to preserve above all else the truth that God alone initiates, sustains and consummates every relationship with fallen humanity.

It is commonplace to hear clergy condemning "decision" theology and criticizing evangelistic crusades such as Billy Graham or evangelical renewal programs such as Promise Keepers. Many Lutheran leaders consciously seek to counter this "heresy" and stamp out the lay people's belief that they can move toward God with a personal commitment.

This strong reaction against the evangelical call for people to "come to Christ" or "make a decision" is understandable. In his commentary on Psalm 90, Luther asserts: "The entire human race fell so far away from God and is so thoroughly blinded by original sin that man knows neither himself nor God."[55] Every confirmed Lutheran learns the third article of *The Apostle's Creed*, which states, "I believe that by my own reason or strength I cannot believe in Jesus Christ, my Lord, or come to him."[56]

At the center of this emphasis is Luther and Calvin's claim that humans, since the fall, have no free will in spiritual matters. The appropriate image used to describe this condition is *blindness*: "The god of this age has blinded the minds of unbelievers, so that they cannot see the light of the gospel of the glory of Christ" (II Corinthians 4:4), and ". . .you were dead in your trespasses and sins, in which you used to live. . ." (Ephesians 2:1). Our theology states unequivocally that we can in no way participate in our salvation or make any move whatsoever toward God. Even our ability to believe in God (faith) is a gift (Ephesians 2:8), given to us by God. The Word and the Spirit are the proud parents of faith in an individual, and they beget their child with no help on our part.

Because of this theological foundation, it is not surprising that Lutheran clergy and theologians gravitate to Biblical verses/passages which emphasize the passivity of the human in the process of salvation. In *The Book of Concord*, *The Solid Declaration* states:

> . . .*Holy Scriptures ascribe conversion, faith in Christ, regeneration, renewal, and everything that belongs to its real beginning and completion in no way to the human powers of the natural free will, be it entirely or one-half or the least and tiniest part, but altogether and alone to the divine operation and the Holy Spirit, as the Apology declares. To some extent reason and free will are able to lead an outwardly virtuous life. But to be born anew, to receive inwardly a new heart, mind, and spirit, is solely the work of the Holy Spirit. He opens the intellect and the heart to understand the Scriptures and to heed the Word, as we read in Luke 24:45, "Then he opened their minds to understand the Scriptures." Likewise, "Lydia heard us; the Lord opened her heart to give heed to what was said by Paul" (Acts 16:14). "For God is at work in you, both to will and to work" (Phil. 2:13). God "gives the repentance" (Acts 5:51, II Tim. 2:25). He works faith, for "It has been granted to you by God that you should believe on him" (Phil. 1:29). "It is the gift of God" (Eph. 2:8). "This is the work of God that you believe in him whom he has sent" (John 6:29). God gives an understanding heart, seeing eyes, and hearing*

ears (Deut. 29:4; Matt. 13:15). The Holy Spirit is a Spirit of regeneration and renewal" (Titus 3:5, 6). God removes the hard stony heart and bestows a new and tender heart of flesh that we may walk in his commandments (Ezek 11:19; 36:26; Deut. 30:6; Ps. 51:12); creates us in Christ Jesus for good works (Eph. 2:10); and makes us new creatures (II Cor. 5:17; Gal. 6:15). In short, every good gift comes from God (James 1:17). No one can come to Christ unless the Father draws him (John 6:44). "No one knows the Father except the Son and any one to whom the Son chooses to reveal him" (Matt. 11:27). "No one can say, Jesus is Lord, except by the Holy Spirit" (I Cor. 12:3). "Apart from me," says Christ, "you can do nothing" (John 15:5). "All our sufficiency is from God" (II Cor. 3:6), "What have you that you did not receive? If then you received it, why do you boast as if it were not a gift?" (1 Cor. 4:7). It was this passage in particular which, by St. Augustine's own statement, persuaded him to recant his former erroneous opinion as he set it forth in his treatise Concerning Predestination... "to assent to this Gospel when it is preached is our own work and lies within our own power." And St. Augustine says further on, "I have erred when I said that it lies within our power to believe and to will, but that it is God's work to give the ability to achieve something to those who believe and will."[57]

Further in the same work we read: "From this we see clearly that the Apology does not ascribe to man's will any ability either to initiate something good or by itself to cooperate."[58]

The problem, however, with placing a strict, one-sided stress on these passages is that much of Scripture also speaks as if humans not only can be but are responsible to respond to God's call through His Word. At first glance these Scriptures seem to contradict the passages quoted above from *The Solid Declaration*. These are the verses that evangelical Christian leaders cling to and use most:

"Seek the Lord while he may be found. . ." (Isaiah 55:6).

"Here I am! I stand at the door and knock. If anyone hears my voice and opens the door, I will come in. . ." (Revelation 3:20).

". . .work out your salvation with fear and trembling. . ." (Philippians 2:12).

"Repent and turn from all your transgressions" (Ezekiel 18:30).

"Cast away from you all your transgressions. . .and get a new heart and a right spirit" (Ezekiel 18:31).

"Let them give up their evil ways. . ." (Jonah 3:8).

". . .'Return to me,' declares the LORD Almighty, 'and I will return to you'. . ." (Zechariah 1:3.).

"Yet to all who received him, to those who believed in his name, he gave the right to become children of God" (John 1:12).

"Come near to God and he will come near to you" (James 4:8).

"Let us draw near to God with a sincere heart. . ." (Hebrews 10:22).

". . .he is able to save completely those who come to God. . ." (Hebrews 7:25).

". . .a better hope is introduced, by which we draw near to God" (Hebrews 7:19).

". . .you received the word of God, which you heard from us, you accepted it. . ." (I Thessalonians 2:13).

> *"Save yourselves from this corrupt generation"* (Acts 2:40).
>
> *"Repent then, and turn to God, so that your sins may be wiped out. . ."* (Acts 3:19).
>
> *". . .they should repent and turn to God. . ."* (Acts 26:20).

Also, in Acts Christian preachers call others to faith by using the imperatives "believe" and "repent," making the hearers think that they are responsible to respond to God.

It cannot suffice to ignore these passages that seem to call for human response and focus solely on those that emphasize human passivity in the process of salvation. Yet it is difficult to comprehend how holding on to both concepts is not clearly contradictory. How can a believer call an unbeliever to respond to God when the believer is sure that unbelievers can do nothing, not even believe, because they are spiritually dead?[59]

Because these two positions seem irreconcilable, most Lutheran pastors feel they have to pick one and reject the other. More often than not, the "passive" is chosen over the "active," a logical choice considering Lutheran doctrine. This instantly erects a wall between us and evangelical clergy because Baptists, Pentecostals, Nazarenes and others have chosen to stress the Scripture verses that imply human involvement. Both camps, in some respects, see the other as an enemy to their own objectives in proclamation. To the Lutheran, the evangelical claim that the human is responsible for salvation through her own decision to believe is at odds with the view that God is the only actor; it obscures the need for Jesus' death as well as minimizes the work of the Holy Spirit. To the Evangelicals, the Lutheran stubbornness in asserting that humans cannot in any way move toward God or respond to Him is a monumental obstacle to evangelism. It is no wonder that Lutheran and Evangelical clergy do not naturally cooperate in mission or dialogue.

While I am proud of the theological clarity and integrity of our Lutheran heritage, I cannot help concluding that when we teach the bondage of the will but refuse to call people to come to Christ, we have failed miserably in some way. People are slipping away from the church and discovering Christ and a spiritual awakening among the evangelicals.

We rarely experience conversions in our midst; even worse, we do not seem to want any. It seems enough for us to tell people that God loves them unconditionally and then baptize them.

I believe the problem is that we do not recognize a paradox at work in the saving process. Could the reality be that on the one hand we can do nothing to move toward God, while on the other hand God expects us to move and holds us responsible to commit to Him? In the Alcoholics Anonymous (AA) philosophy, a person who is an alcoholic is controlled by an addiction over which he cannot by his own power or will escape. That person is in fact unable to make a decision to change and succeed. At the same time, AA does not conclude that people are thus not responsible for their actions. The opposite is true. The individual is called to take full responsibility for his failures and sins.

I believe that there is something good and necessary in both the Lutheran adherence to no free will for the individual and the evangelical call to faith that makes an individual seem to be approaching God through his own decision and commitment. I think they both are true positions, and perhaps both are necessary for God to do His work properly. I believe Jesus is both God *and* man. I can certainly believe in the coexistence of divine sovereignty *and* human response.

TECHNICAL AND PSYCHOLOGICAL LANGUAGE

A colleague, with whom I once worked, expressed frustration and some anger at those evangelicals who taught that a person had to make a decision for Christ or accept Christ to be saved. His consternation is echoed in the minds of countless other Lutheran clergy. I, having many evangelical friends who use such language, sought to defend them. I know they also believe it is by grace that a person is saved, and without the activity of the Holy Spirit it is impossible for an individual to believe. I argued the very fact that Billy Graham's organization demands large-scale prayer for each crusade (starting at least a year beforehand), proves that they believe their efforts in calling people to make a decision are useless without the work of God through the Holy Spirit. In other words, many people who call an individual to "accept" Christ believe that the person cannot in reality accept Christ without being opened up to God by the Spirit's activity. My friend replied, "Then, why don't they say what they mean?"

"Why don't they say what they mean?" That is a good question. If one believes a person cannot make a decision for Christ, then how can he use a false statement that implies the contrary? This all seems logical enough, and I do not blame clergy who refuse to use language that in their minds is not true. The problem, however, is that language has the flexibility of being both true and not true simultaneously. Not realizing this is what makes fundamentalists assert something that is untenable to Lutherans, namely that the Bible should be taken literally. But this same mistake is at work when we claim that we cannot call people to decide, accept or believe in Christ because the Bible says that they are not able to respond to God. And yet, the church throughout the ages, as well as the Apostles in Acts talk to unbelievers as if their salvation depends on their own response and does not refrain from calling people to move toward the Almighty.

What is going on here is the ability of language to speak on different levels, and the possibility of language being untrue in one aspect while true in another. Language can explain technical truth or psychological truth, but when focusing on one of these aspects it may by its very nature be false concerning the other.

Let me give a non-theological example. Meteorologists who give the weather reports on television often say something like, "The sun will rise at 6:15 tomorrow morning." If we expected the scientifically-trained professional to always be technically accurate, we would be disappointed, because it is technically wrong to say that the sun rises. In truth, the sun does not move at all. It is the earth that moves (rotates). So, why is a meteorologist making a false statement? If we Lutheran clergy were consistent with how we respond to this statement compared to the way we respond to the theologically false claim that an individual moves toward God in salvation, we would be very upset. We would probably turn the television off and maybe write a stern letter to the station, scolding them for hiring a meteorologist who makes obviously false statements to the public. We know the meteorologist understands that the sun doesn't move, so our question might be, "Why doesn't he say what he means?"

The misunderstanding here has to do with the versatility of language. It can convey both a technical and a psychological truth. Technical truth is a statement relating what empirically or objectively happens: the earth rotates. Psychological truth relates the reality of what one experiences subjectively. From our perspective on this earth, we see the sun moving across the sky as the day progresses. To say "the sun rises" or "the sun sets" may not be so much a false statement as a true psychological statement. In fact, from our perspective, the sun is definitely the object that moves.

The same meteorologist may also give two temperatures: the mercury reading and the wind-chill. Is one truer than the other? I believe that they are both true, one technically (mercury reading) and one psychologically (wind-chill). If the mercury reads +5°, but the wind chill reads -35°, I dare a person to dress for the former in an attempt to prove that the warmer temperature is the true, objective reality. From the individual's subjective perspective and his senses, the temperature will feel like -35°. He will be sorry if he ignores the subjective reality and instead dresses for the warmer temperature.

If both technical truth and psychological language help explain everyday reality, why should we not assume that it is a helpful distinction in the theological world as well? In fact, it is because we often fail to make this distinction regarding how the Gospel is proclaimed and received that we often lose the power of it.

Maybe the evangelical crying, "Accept Christ!" and the Lutheran scholar muttering, "You can do nothing in the saving process!" are not conveying opposing and contradictory statements. Maybe they are instead complementary and helpful in different enterprises, one for proclamation and the other for instruction. Could it be that the call to move toward God is better couched in psychological words that speak of it from the perspective of the hearer? To the one listening, it will seem from her vantage-point that she is moving toward God. Yet, if analyzed technically, we would have to admit that the Holy Spirit silently, mysteriously and completely calls, moves and persuades the heart of the hearer even though she may not sense it.

The sun does move across the sky as we watch it from the surface of the earth. Objectively, we understand that in fact the sun does not move at all, but instead it is the earth that is rotating. However, we do not sense that we have experienced a loss of integrity when we make the statement "the sun rises" or "the sun sets." It is acceptable and even helpful to explain psychological reality. Likewise, when speaking about conversion, it is indeed acceptable and healthy to speak of it as the person "coming to Christ," or "making a decision for Christ." From the individual's perspective, he did make a decision to move toward God in his heart and mind. This neither negates nor blemishes the technical reality that God started, maintained and completed the work Himself in a spiritually dead and blind person.

Many Lutheran leaders have seemingly backed themselves into a corner with the misunderstanding that they can only use technical, theologically correct language when talking about the faith. The limitation this conclusion brings is paralyzing. It would be similar to a scientist who wants to communicate his deep feelings of love for his wife, but who is unwilling to give up technical language for more poetic words because he thinks that the statements and images in that genre are not technically true. If we do not use psychological language, we will not be able to speak to people in any deeply meaningful way.

It seems to me that psychological language is used in the Scriptures when a believer seeks to move unbelieving hearts toward God. In Acts, the Apostles did not use technical language when trying to share the Gospel so that the Spirit might work faith in unbelievers. It would be unfortunate if they were limited to such language. Can you imagine them saying, "Please listen to me, but do not try and do anything because you are not able to. When you hear the Gospel, do not accept it or think that you can repent." On the other hand, Acts also speaks in places to the reader using technical statements which claim that those who believe can only do so because they were drawn to God by the Holy Spirit.

Apparently, the Holy Spirit prefers psychological language when seeking to work faith in people. That may explain why few people experience conversion in the Lutheran church, while thousands are converted at an evangelistic crusade where there is a specific call given to people, urging them to respond to the Gospel. Technical language is necessary and should follow as a convert matures in understanding his experience and God's invisible activity in the saving process.

Perhaps the Presbyterian Church USA in their *A Declaration of Faith* has the right balance when they state:

> *The Spirit enabled people. . .to accept the good news of what God has done in Christ, repent of their sins, and enter the community of faith. We testify that today the same Holy Spirit makes us able to respond in faith to the gospel. . .The Spirit makes us aware of our sinfulness and need, moves us to abandon our old way of life, persuades us to trust in Christ and adopt his way. In all these things we are responsible for our decisions. But after we have trusted and repented we*

> *recognize that the Spirit enabled us to hear and act. It is not our faith but God's grace in Jesus Christ that justifies us and reconciles us to God. Yet it is only by faith that we accept God's grace and live by it.*[60]

Here we have a nice balance between the subjective experience of the individual and the objective reality of it.

Lutherans will continue to be paralyzed in the area of bearing witness to the Gospel in any effective way to the world if they do not regain the ability to use psychological language in proclamation. We may also have to drop the unconscious additive, "People are saved by grace through faith *plus* a perfect understanding at the time of conversion or awakening of how the saving process works." We must be patient and use technical verbiage only after an individual has saving faith. Let the Spirit work faith through our call for a person to respond. Later, as the person lives in the community of faith, we can share with him (and remind all others) of the unseen force of the Spirit which controlled the saving process from start to finish.

PARADOX 1

God: Three and One

The beginning of *The Augsburg Confession* starts with the article concerning God. It says:

> *We unanimously hold and teach, in accordance with the decree of the Council of Nicaea, that there is one divine essence, which is called and which is truly God, and that there are three persons in this one divine essence, equal in power and alike eternal: God the Father, God the Son, God the Holy Spirit. All three are one divine essence, eternal, without division, without end, of infinite power, wisdom, and goodness, one creator and preserver of all things visible and invisible.*[61]

The doctrine of the Trinity has been a core Christian belief from the first centuries. Because it describes such a profound mystery, we are severely restricted in our articulation of it. Suffice it to say that the doctrine is the fruit of a faithful reading of the Scriptures.

God is Father, Son and Holy Spirit. We also say that God is Creator, Savior and Paraclete. I like to think that the doctrine of the Trinity communicates the invisible presence of God in the world (Father), the visible presence of God in the world (Son), and the intimate presence of God in the human believer (Spirit). Each person of the Trinity communicates God's presence to humans in varying forms of intimacy in order to provide physical life, spiritual salvation and daily guidance.

God, the Creator/Father, is constantly active in and through the natural processes in order to provide life for humans. This invisible presence manifests itself through physical elements. In the Old Testament at Mt. Sinai, Moses had the Hebrew people build a tabernacle from plans God gave to him on the mountain. When completed, a "...cloud covered the Tent of Meeting, and the glory of the Lord filled the tabernacle" (Exodus 40:34). A cloud was seen around the tabernacle, not God Himself. That invisible presence works mysteriously in creation, often unacknowledged by people, in order to care for the creation He loves. God, who is not an element of the universe, works through the elements of the universe to bring life. From a human perspective water and sun make the crops grow. But it is the invisible presence of God and His blessing that brings life to us through the food that grows. It is natural for humans to conclude that a man and a woman create the miracle of new life. Yet we believe that God is the primary cause of all life begun and preserved.

Because of human sin and separation from God, God had to move closer to humanity in order to redeem them. In fact, He had to break into time and space and take on human flesh. The Gospel of John says: "The Word became flesh and made his dwelling among us. We have seen his glory, the glory of the One and Only, who came from the Father, full of grace and truth" (1:14). Jesus Himself declares: "I and the Father are one" (John 10:30). The incarnation is God becoming physically present in the world He created. He actually becomes an element of the universe that He made. God suddenly communicated to humanity in a visible presence, able to be seen, touched and heard. Only as a human was He able to redeem other humans from the curse of their spiritual death. As God's invisible presence was most clearly communicated in the Old Testament Tent of Meeting, God's visible presence was communicated most profoundly through Jesus' human body.

God the Spirit represents God's most intimate communication to humans, a communication that penetrates into the human himself in a most intimate manner. In I Corinthians, Paul asks, "Don't you know that you yourselves are God's temple and that God's Spirit lives in you?" (3:16). In the Old Testament God's invisible presence was found pitched in a tent of canvas. In Jesus, God 'pitches his tent' in a human body. His Spirit now "pitches" the divine presence intimately in humans. As invisible Father, He works through all things created in order to provide His world with life. As visible Son, He Himself becomes part of creation in order to give humans spiritual life. Then as intimate Spirit, God inhabits human beings in order to gain a permanent and ongoing presence in His world in order to use us to do His work. The Trinity communicates, above all, that God gives Himself to humanity in order to provide everything needed for life.

It is essential for the church to cling to a Trinitarian understanding of God's communication to humanity in order to avoid a truncated view of God's person and work. Yet it is an easy temptation for any denomination to focus on the work of one person of the Trinity while neglecting the others. It seems that some Baptist denominations, as well as many other Evangelical ones, may be tempted to focus on the second person of the Trinity over and above the first and third. The temptation for many Pentecostal churches may be to over-emphasize the third person over the first and second. As for most main-line denominations, it seems that focus on the first person of the Trinity is the tendency today.

What happens when one person of the Trinity is overemphasized? Or perhaps better stated, what happens when others are neglected? If it is the first person that is stressed to the exclusion of the others, much good can come. With its emphasis on creation and God's unseen involvement in everything that brings physical life, the church will seek to care for the poor, work for justice and care for the environment. This is the natural fruit of a belief that God is the Creator of all that is, and that humans have the power to aid Him in nurturing life and health as well as to destroy it. This world is a beautiful gift from God, and we are His caretakers and stewards. This life, this body and this world all have great significance and value.

But if the second and third persons are neglected, one can easily slip into a materialism where the spiritual world and spiritual needs of people, including reconciliation with God through faith in Jesus Christ, are minimized. Jesus may be held up as a model for faithful living in creation, but not presented as the Savior who heals spiritual brokenness and sin.

One pastor friend of mine is deeply involved with inner-city ministries seeking to care for the poor and voiceless. He is part of a group of people seeking to help refugees with often-neglected needs in the American city in which he lives. He cares for people who are weak and needy in many other ways as well. When I am fortunate enough to see him, I am inspired by his love for God's world and for the people He created. I see in him a healthy understanding of God as Creator. But he shows little concern for the spiritual development of the people in his congregation. It seems to be his goal to encourage his members to serve God in the physical world, as he does.

On the other hand, I unconsciously stress the second person of the Trinity and the salvation of souls more than the other two persons. When my friend and I get together, I feel as if we complement each other. As he relates his ministry to me, I cannot help but sense a failure on my part to live with a healthier respect for God as Creator. I hope that my focus on evangelism may also encourage him to take a greater look at the second person of the Trinity.

Though Lutheranism has traditionally been known as a second-person denomination, it seems to me that the ELCA has moved, along with most mainline denominations, toward a strong theology based on the first person. It seems that Jesus and faith in Him have in many ways been left behind.

When I graduated from Luther Northwestern Seminary thirteen years ago, my evangelical siblings attended the ceremony at Central Lutheran Church in Minneapolis, Minnesota. After the event they asked me why the name Jesus was not mentioned in the half-hour homily. I attempted to justify this important absence. As the years have passed, however, I have become more curious about this fact. It now seems significant to me that Jesus was not mentioned in the sermon of a seminary graduation, where the church was sending out pastors to proclaim and celebrate the risen Lord.

I have noticed Jesus' absence in many other places in the church. A number of years ago, I decided to take the most recent publication of *The Lutheran* and look for the name of Jesus. In over thirty pages, the name Jesus or Lord appeared only a couple times in the articles but always parenthetically (e.g. ". . .the prayer Jesus taught us"). The only time the name Jesus was used in its own right was in a back page article talking about Baptists around the country having block parties in order to evangelize. The article said that the goal was to bring people to Jesus Christ.

The stories in *The Lutheran* that month had an overwhelming first-person emphasis. Physical needs around the world were addressed. Politics in third world countries, poverty in various places and natural disasters that had devastated certain places were all the major stories. This is all wonderful and reflects God's concern for the earth, the environment and people in any kind of suffering or need. But the absence of talk about faith in Jesus was striking.

That edition of *The Lutheran* also recapped the most recent ELCA national convention. The highlights of the assembly, along with the items discussed and resolutions passed and defeated, were addressed. It was good to see much discussion on how to better care for the poor, the neglected and the environment. But there was no evidence that the convention was concerned in the least about evangelism. That topic was not even addressed.

The synod assemblies I have attended over the past fifteen years have also been exemplary in their concern for needy people in the world, encouraging those present to be more concerned about social concerns and the poor. But I have to admit that I do not recall much emphasis on the need to share the Gospel with those who do not know Jesus Christ. I consider both this example and the consistent content of our denomination's publications as strong proof that our church is definitely first-person heavy, while severely neglecting the second person and evangelism.

The lack of call to faith in Jesus Christ and the absence of encouragement to share the faith are also obvious in educational materials, Sunday school curriculum and the themes of books being published by our publishing houses. It is possible now for our children to go through the entire Sunday school and confirmation process and not hear about the need to share Christ with others. Most youth I have observed in the church do not even know that people without faith in Christ are in need of the Gospel.

Missionary support in the ELCA has steadily declined since its inception in the late 1980s. Our denomination of 10,000 congregations now supports fewer than 300 missionaries. On the other hand, our denomination has been involved in many social issues, has fought for political justice in many ways, has been on the scene to care for people in the aftermath of natural disasters, has demonstratively preached against prejudice of any form and has constantly reminded us of God's call to help the poor and voiceless. I say the latter with great pride in our denomination. We do understand well the first-person position. We have embraced this world and the care for the needy because of our understanding that this is God's world and His people. But we have conversely been just as poor at evangelism.

If we continue to serve God in the world without centering that service in the salvation we have obtained through the death and resurrection of Jesus Christ, we ultimately will be no different from any other human organization working for the common good. If we neglect evangelism, we will be keeping people from the single most important element they lack in this life: a relationship, through faith, with the risen Lord Jesus Christ. Sharing Christ Jesus and encouraging spiritual reconciliation to God through Christ is the one unique task of the church. We cannot fail here.

It seems to me that our denomination also lacks a strong third-person theology. This shows among us pastors. When we come out of seminary, we are more prepared to run a church on our own than we are to seek the Holy

Spirit's guidance and help in the process. We have not been trained to pray, to discern God's presence in our midst or to listen to God. Consequently, we are tempted to take control of a congregation and run it like a CEO or a manager would run a business.

It has taken me over a decade of ministry to begin to learn how to depend upon and trust in the ever-active presence of the Holy Spirit. I have come to realize that I naturally do God's work as if I were the only one involved. I so often completely fail to comprehend the power and working of the Spirit. It also struck me recently that I build a vision for a congregation and then proceed on my own initiative, while rarely asking God what He desires. It is possible to hear God's voice and discern His direction more than we have been taught. It may not be easy. It may take time and a lot of practice. But it is the difference between depending upon our own powers and skills, and depending upon the Spirit.

I have only begun to learn how to follow God, trust in the Spirit's guidance and listen for His leading. I imagine I will be learning the rest of my life. I know that I am heading in the right direction. In other words, I am inserting a Biblical theology of the third person into my ministry, something I lacked before. I am letting go of my need to control affairs. I am more aware of God's dealings even in the failures and flops of my ministry. I am learning that God can work as much through my weaknesses as He can through my strengths. I am gaining an understanding that adequate preparation for my sermon should include much prayer, as well as manuscript work.

The absence of prayer among many groups of clergy, as well as in many pastor's personal lives, may betray a poor understanding of the third person and the Spirit's work. I am coming to understand more and more that few pastors I know have a prayer life of quality or quantity. I must admit that I struggle in this respect as well. Maybe it is because we have a greater confidence in what we can achieve than we do in what the Spirit can achieve.

I have also been discouraged by how few lay people are trained in prayer, especially those under the age of fifty. In my present congregation, I have found it virtually impossible to find a handful of praying individuals who feel comfortable enough to commit to praying, either on Sunday morning for the worship services or regularly for the church in general. I understand that part of this is due to shyness. But perhaps another part of it is that we as pastors have been poor at teaching prayer or emphasizing its importance.

I think that our temptation is to pass on our own person-centered work ethic to lay people. What I mean is the work ethic that depends upon our efforts for things to be accomplished. We as pastors seem inclined to act instead of pray, to depend upon our accomplishments instead of trusting the Spirit, and to value getting something done more than waiting for God.

We probably pass on this attitude to our congregations. We may tend to emphasize serving God in the world by doing helpful acts (as we should), but we may fail to teach people how to involve the Spirit in the process or how to listen to His leading.

The best way I can think of to help renew a healthy respect for and an understanding of the work of the second and third persons of the Trinity is to dialogue and spend time with other Christian denominations which emphasize these and have a healthy theology of them. For instance, we might want to explore ways in which certain Baptist denominations approach evangelism. We may want to explore how the Assembly of God denomination encourages its people to use gifts of the Spirit.

When we dialogue only with like-minded denominations, we usually share many of the same strengths and weaknesses. The relationship may be more natural and easier, but we may glean less. By reaching out to diverse denominations in dialogue, we may be able to gain a healthier understanding of many things we often neglect, including the second and third persons of the Trinity.

I believe that it is typical for every denomination to be drawn to one person and work of the Trinity more than to the others. Yet, this should not keep us from trying to be more holistic, and as a result more healthy and balanced.

PARADOX 2

Jesus: God and Man

The third article of *The Augsburg Confession* entitled "Concerning the Son of God" states:

> *It is also taught among us that God the Son became man, born of the virgin Mary, and that the two natures, divine and human, are so inseparably united in one person that there is one Christ, true God and true man, who was truly born, suffered, was crucified, died, and was buried in order to be a sacrifice not only for original sin but also for all other sins and to propitiate God's wrath.*[62]

The paradox of Jesus is that He is God and man at the same time. Since the first centuries, the church has vehemently opposed any doctrine that denies in any way or minimizes either Jesus' humanity or His divinity. It is essential to hold both truths tightly together if anything else we say about Jesus and His work will be true.

My first inclination when writing this piece was to leave out this paradox. In fact, it did not even cross my mind to place it here. I assumed that this is one doctrine that all pastors believed as a matter of course. However, after years of talks with clergy I have become more and more aware that it is not so much that they deny its truth, but that few pastors have seriously addressed this topic, many times not even at seminary. Consequently, errors in theology arise that could have been avoided if the ramifications of such a doctrine were clearly understood.

I exited seminary without a thorough understanding of where the doctrine of Jesus' two natures were founded Biblically. I knew more of what the debates on this issue were throughout the centuries than what the Scriptures actually stated. It was not until my persistent encounter with

Jehovah's Witnesses in parish ministry that I began to search the Scriptures for myself to see what they said concerning Jesus' divinity.

The Bible is consistent about its claim that Jesus is God. The Gospel of John's preoccupation with that claim makes us think that many Christians at the time were tempted to disregard Jesus' divinity. John begins his Gospel with the words, "In the beginning was the Word, and the Word was with God, and the Word was God" (John 1:1).

In John 8:58, Jesus exclaims, "I am!" God, in the third chapter of Exodus, calls Himself the same. To the Jews who were listening to Jesus at the time, this was a clear identification with God. In fact, they took up stones to kill him for blasphemy. Two chapters later, Jesus claims, "I and the Father are one" (John 10:30). Again the Jews wanted to stone him. Jesus asked why. They responded that it was because of blasphemy, ". . .because you, a mere man, claim to be God" (John 10:33b). It is clear that the Jews heard Jesus claim to be divine.

Paul is clear about Jesus' divinity:

> *He is the image of the invisible God. . .For by him all things were created (Colossians 1:15, 16).*
>
> *For in Christ all the fullness of the Deity lives in bodily form. . . (Colossians 2:9).*
>
> *. . .Christ Jesus: Who, being in very nature God. . . (Philippians 2:6a).*

The author of Hebrews states: "The Son is the radiance of God's glory and the exact representation of his being. . ." (1:3). In the Gospel of John, Thomas beholds the risen Lord for the first time and exclaims, "My Lord and my God!" (20:28). In Revelation 22:1, God the Creator shares His throne with the Lamb (Jesus). Also in Revelation, Jesus calls Himself names that were previously reserved only for God: "I am the Alpha and the Omega, the First and the Last, the Beginning and the End" (22:13).

There are many more Scriptures that point to the divinity of Jesus, but the above selections make it clear that the Bible states unequivocally that Jesus is God. Throughout the centuries, the church has clung to this belief simply because it is scriptural. The Bible states that Jesus is divine as well as human.

I believe that the significance of this truth has been lost on many church leaders today. And yet, without this all-important doctrine, the basis of Christian faith collapses. Without it our reason for witnessing to Jews and Muslims evaporates.

The doctrine that ultimately divides Christians from other serious theists is that Jesus is God, as well as man. We believe that this truth holds the secret to life with God.

Why is the doctrine of the two natures of Jesus Christ so essential? The answer is this: it draws out the reality of sin and its absolute power to ruin human relationship with God. Like Muslims and Jews, we believe that humans fail morally and stumble before the holy God. Like them, we believe that this sin separates us from the Almighty. Where we part ways, however, is on the question of sin's seriousness. All three religions believe that human sin is serious, but only Christians believe that it is so serious that it has completely paralyzed humanity spiritually, keeping them from ever regaining a redemptive relationship with God through their own efforts.

Only Christianity believes that sin so completely destroyed humanity's relationship with God that He had to come in person to remedy the problem. Only God could make right what sin had so totally severed. Only God could present a final solution that would rectify this human/divine separation: appear in the flesh (incarnation) and destroy sin's stranglehold by dying on a cross and rising again.

Let me explain. I have no mechanical abilities whatsoever. I do not know how to fix appliances or electronic devices, no matter how small the problem. I do not know how to get the computer going again after a glitch stops my work. I do not know how to make even simple repairs on our house. My wife, on the other hand, is extremely mechanical. She can understand problems with electronic devices and knows how to find a way of getting the computer going again. Anything I can do, she can do better, when it comes to mechanical things.

Consequently, if I come home and see a van in our driveway from a local electrical or plumbing business, I know that there is something wrong in our home that neither Kay nor I can fix. Because we are helpless at times to repair something, we have to call in experts who can do it. In the same way, when I look at the truth that God took on human form in Jesus, I instantly know that something must have been so seriously wrong with the relationship we have with God that only He could repair it.

Christianity rejects the notion that most theistic religions hold: that a human can perform certain good deeds or participate in enough religious rituals to merit a renewed relationship with God. Instead, we teach that while we can do nothing to improve our broken relationship with God, He can and does choose to repair it anyway. It is by grace that we are saved. Salvation is an absolute gift to sinners who can never change enough to satisfy what sin has lost for us.

Today, pastors of mainline churches often focus on the humanity of Jesus to the neglect of His divinity. This happens by holding up Jesus as a good role model for us in our search to be what God wants us to be. Jesus, the man, gives us the best example of what a human life should be.

Jesus' divinity is minimized at times for at least two reasons. One is that many pastors are uncomfortable with the thought that Jesus is God. It may simply seem too difficult a concept to swallow. It may seem too good to be true! Secondly, many are embarrassed by this doctrine because it divides us from other theists whom we respect. If it weren't for the theology of Jesus' divinity, there would be very few obstacles in the way of a deep unity with Muslims, Jews and others. So for the sake of unity and for the appearance of being tolerant, we often minimize Jesus' divinity and advocate instead His humanity.

The problem with focusing only on Jesus' humanity is that the Scriptures and the Lutheran confessions state without shame that He is both God *and* man. That means that Jews, Muslims and many others have an incomplete picture of human nature as well as of the depth of God's grace. In spite of their good intentions to love and follow God, they remain spiritually separated from Him because they have not yet embraced the remedy God has offered: Jesus Christ, dead and risen, and faith in His name.

Because Jesus is divine, we know our sins are too much for us. We understand that we were helpless to find God before the incarnation. We believe that this great gift of reconciliation is only accomplished through Jesus and faith in Him. Thus, while we can celebrate unity on many issues with other theists, we cannot unequivocally state that they are brothers and sisters in faith. We are called to supplement the many correct thoughts about God with the one thought that is essential: humans are separated from God and are utterly incapable of pleasing Him unto salvation. But God has offered Himself in Christ, opening the way to life with Himself for those who trust in the redemptive work of Jesus to redeem them from their sin and separation.

PARADOX 3

Christians: Saints and Sinners

Lutheran theology distinguishes two realities of the regenerated person: saint and sinner. We become saints because of a happy exchange: we give Jesus our sin, and He gives us His righteousness. Unfortunately, our sinful nature remains.

In the *Large Catechism*, Luther states: ". . .confession should and must take place incessantly as long as we live. For this is the essence of a genuinely Christian life, to acknowledge that we are sinners and to pray for grace."[63] When speaking about the Lord's Supper, Luther says: ". . .they alone are unworthy who neither feel their infirmities nor admit to being sinners."[64] Elsewhere Luther states:

> *We live in the flesh and we have the old Adam hanging around our necks; he goes to work and lures us daily into unchastity, laziness, gluttony and drunkenness, greed and deceit, into acts of fraud and deception against our neighbor—in short, into all kinds of evil lusts which by nature cling to us and to which we are incited by the association and example of other people and by things we hear and see.*[65]

The tendency for clergy of the ELCA has been to fall on the saint side of the paradox and to minimize instruction to the faithful concerning ongoing sin. This, I believe, is for several reasons. First of all, most of our clergy are pastoral-sensitive and want to help members gain a healthy emotional attitude. This includes a love for self and an awareness of God's great love for them. Talk of sin can be seen as a possible obstacle to this.

Secondly, I believe our clergy are reacting to what they perceive as destructive in much of the preaching and teaching about sin among many conservative denominations and churches. Many clergy believe a "hellfire and brimstone" approach to sin is still prevalent among evangelicals and fundamentalists, and they consciously or unconsciously gravitate toward a neglect of speaking about sin in order to counter this threat to people's "healthy relationship" to God.

Thirdly, where a universalism or "infant baptism saves adults" theology is present among pastors, sin is no longer seen as a problem. It is not as necessary to speak of the believer as sinner because that sinful nature is not and cannot be a threat to their relationship with God. It is thought that the old Adam does not threaten salvation.

The problem is that a paradox needs both pillars of the married truths in order to stand. If one side is heavily favored in preaching and teaching, and the other minimized or neglected, truth will at some point be compromised. In this case, believers who are not instructed carefully about the power of the old Adam to turn a believer's heart away from God may become complacent in Christian life and have a false confidence that all was completed by God once and for all.

It is a small exaggeration to say that at a couple of text studies I have attended, it seemed that some clergy present simply wanted to find a way to preach, from every text, the news that all those listening were saints, that is, baptized and therefore with God. Neglected often is the truth that the saints are at the same time sinners, and the old nature poses a real threat to an ongoing relationship with God. Most preaching seeks to bless the hearers with the news that they are saints through God's grace. As a result, masses of people leave church on Sunday morning feeling good about themselves even if they are not right with God. They have little challenge or warning to beware of the old nature that clings so tightly and seeks to daily usurp the new creation.

No wonder that there are relatively few people in most of our congregations who read the Bible or earnestly pray! If there are no dangers or threats to the life of faith, what incentive is there to do anything to protect it? If there are no enemies that threaten our relationship with God, then there is little reason to arm ourselves.

But the confessions clearly teach that faith is at all times vulnerable to three constant enemies: self (sin), Satan and society (where it is opposed to God). They clearly teach that one's faith can be destroyed if neglected. In Luther's comments on the second commandment in the *Large Catechism*, he talks about "...the devil, who is ever around us, lying in wait to lure us into sin and shame, calamity and trouble."[66] Also in the *Large Catechism*, speaking about the third commandment, Luther says:

> ...*the devil bewitches and befuddles the hearts of many so that he may take us by surprise and stealthily take the Word of God away from us. Let me tell you this. Even though you know the Word perfectly and have already mastered everything, still you are daily under the dominion of the devil, who neither day nor night relaxes his effort to steal upon you unawares and to kindle in your heart unbelief and wicked thoughts...Therefore you must continually keep God's Word in your heart, on your lips, and in your ears. For where the heart stands idle and the Word is not heard, the devil breaks in and does his damage before we realize it.*[67]

In the preface to his *Large Catechism*, Luther speaks clearly about the terrible enemies that beset us:

> ...*knows our danger and need. He knows the constant and furious attacks and assaults of the devil. So he wishes to warn, equip, and protect us against them with good "armor" against their "flaming darts" and with a good antidote against their evil infection and poison. O what mad, senseless fools we are! We must ever live and dwell in the midst of such mighty enemies as the devils, and yet we despise our weapons and armor, too lazy to give them a thought!*[68]

The confessions constantly warn against overpowering enemies that not only hinder our service to God but also threaten our faith and salvation. If we expunge all mention of Satan and the old Adam from the confessions, so much no longer makes sense. However, in our preaching and teaching we often avoid talk of sin and of Satan as well as of warnings about the damage each can do to our faith.

The countless warnings about Satan in our confessions are actually indictments against the sinful nature that clings to us. It is because we are sinners, oriented toward self and vulnerable to corruption and deception, that the devil is such a threat. Throughout our earthly existence, we will remain sinners and in need of constant help and ongoing forgiveness to retain the faith. As a result, we desperately need regular prayer, Bible reading and study, Christian fellowship and the bread and wine.

There is a glaring absence among our people (especially those under fifty) of a real concern about tending their faith. This has come partly because clergy have not convinced them of the seriousness of their ongoing sin and of the dangerous enemies that could pull them away from a redemptive relationship with God. Consequently, the spiritual disciplines (prayer, Bible reading, etc.) are becoming low priorities for even serious Christians.

Christian faith is like a garden: it needs constant tending because it is vulnerable to enemies. Even though faith is planted (baptism) and growing (through contact with Word and sacrament), it is always vulnerable to forces that seek its destruction and to things that divert our attention to caring for that faith. Enemies of a garden are rabbits and deer, lack of rain, too much rain, poor soil, frost and weeds. In the same way our sinful nature, Satan and segments of society are enemies that can cause serious damage to our faith, and if neglected for too long, can destroy it altogether.

Many years ago I waited too long to plant pea seeds in my garden. I was told by a friend to put the seeds in a bowl of water where they would germinate quickly. I did this and watched the seeds germinate and sprout. Then I planted the seeds in the garden where the soil could nurture them. If I had kept the seeds in the water indefinitely, they would have died. They need the soil to survive.

Likewise, we should refuse to baptize children of parents who have no visible connection to God and the church. It would be like throwing pea seeds into water and leaving them there to die. In baptism, even with children of non-believing parents, germination of faith takes place. Relationship with God begins and sprouts because of God's Word and the elements. If the child is not "planted" in the church, the "soil" that nurtures faith through Word and sacrament, then that child's faith will ultimately die. We should be just as adamantly opposed to baptizing these children as we are to throwing seeds in a bowl of water and leaving them there to die. When we baptize children, we are negligent if we fail to warn the parents that even when the baptized child is connected immediately to the church and God's Word, there are great and powerful forces that will work against that child's faith and that could in the end steal it or destroy it. It has been my experience that a majority of parents who baptize their children give little or no thought of the serious dangers that lie ahead for their child's faith. Consequently, I rarely observe parents who are worried enough about the possibility of their baptized child losing his relationship with God down the road that they take it upon themselves to aggressively nurture the child's faith at home. It is uncommon for a vast majority of these young families to have regular devotions, read Bible stories to their children or teach their children how to pray. Most of these parents even regard church attendance for worship as having minimal importance and being low on the totem pole of priorities.

From where does this apathy come? I believe that the church has a part to play in it. In many and various ways some clergy stress the fact that the baptized are saints because of Jesus' death and resurrection, although we may not use the term "saint" explicitly. Our talk of baptism can at least sound like it is an act that completes our transformation from separation from God to child of God once and for all. Clergy may not articulate the above notions in the above language, but it is communicated nevertheless. We have often failed to remind people that all who are baptized are still sinners and thus susceptible to many dangers and enemies that can in fact destroy faith.

One of our worst short-comings in many of our confirmation programs is our failure to adequately convince our young people that they are sinners. Many times we do not even try! One of the most difficult things about teaching a paradoxical truth is that we often feel that one half of the paradox (we are sinners) can work against our argument for the other half (we are saints). As a result we often emphasize one side while neglecting the other.

Clergy often emphasize baptism, stressing it as the event where God incorporated us into His family (made us saints). But confirmation students often fail to develop a good understanding that they are sinners. In fact, most never get the message, and as adults they have little idea of the seriousness of their present sin and sinful condition.

One serious consequence of this failure to convince our young people that they are sinners is that we fail to prepare them for a life of ongoing repentance. If they think they are "not so bad," or if they deny their sinfulness, they will have no inclination or disposition to admit their sin to God. This in turn becomes critical because without repentance, the benefits of baptism (forgiveness, relationship with God and eternal life) will be lost. We honor baptism only through our ongoing repentance.

The Solid Declaration is blunt about this truth, ". . .there cannot be genuine saving faith in those who live without contrition and sorrow and have a wicked intention to remain and abide in sin, for true contrition precedes and genuine faith exists only in or with true repentance."[69]

If we fail to convince our people of their sin (saints though they are), we also fail to instruct them about how to properly prepare for the sacrament. *The Solid Declaration* states:

> *. . .the body and blood of Christ are truly distributed to the unworthy, too, and that they truly receive it. But they receive it for judgment, as St. Paul says, for they misuse the holy sacrament since they receive it without true repentence and without faith.*[70]

My colleagues often criticize our Missouri Synod counterparts for emphasizing the sin of the communion recipient (thus often keeping visitors from the sacrament because the local pastor cannot know their faithfulness to God or know them well enough to sense a repentant heart), instead of emphasizing God's grace bestowed in the bread and wine.

Yet, the Lutheran confessions seem to agree that we should not bestow communion on everyone indiscriminately, implying that all are saints just because they eat and drink the elements. We instead should adamantly teach our congregations that the Lord's Supper should only be received by those who truly are repentant. It would not be too difficult to say something to that effect, in a gentle manner, before the elements are distributed. It is irresponsible not to make this clear. The pastor could simply say that all are welcome at the table if they are truly repentant of their sins. I am not naïve enough to believe that most people who are even aware of their unwillingness to repent will stay in their pew when all around them are going forward for the bread and wine. In some cases it could be very embarrassing. If only the clergy could communicate clearly that communion is only for the repentant; it is not up to that pastor to guess at who is and is not presently repenting (unless a member is openly and publicly sinning with willful intent). In teaching our members this truth, we instruct them about their constant sinfulness and need for repentance.

Many clergy are nervous about emphasizing to young people (or adults for that matter) that they are sinners. This is understandable because there is a massive precedence of millions of people who have faced deep despair in the false conviction that their sin was greater than God's ability or willingness to forgive. Many people are also susceptible to a self-condemnation that becomes an obstacle to them, preventing them from comprehending God's mercy and love for them. It is a difficult challenge to convince people of their sin, while at the same time keeping them away from the abyss of a destructive self-image or a preoccupation with the false belief that they need to be a better person or do certain things before they are acceptable to God.

Yet, we cannot abandon the project of communicating the reality of both saint and sinner. To do so leads to misconceptions among lay people that can greatly confuse a proper understanding of their relationship with God. I believe that there are ways for clergy to help distinguish between Christians as sinners, and at the same time, as made in God's image. We should be able to communicate that they are intrinsically valuable without abandoning the call for continual repentance. In my first pastoral call, a sincere Christian woman expressed confusion over the Biblical description of humans as made in God's image in some places and talk of all people as terrible sinners in others. In the past, this woman had done numerous things for which she was terribly ashamed. Added to that, she had been physically and verbally abused by her first husband. She also was in an ongoing ministry with other abused women. She knew first-hand how devastating Christian views about human sinfulness can be when they are misunderstood.

I must admit that I did not know how to answer this woman. I realized that I myself was confused about it. I know my confusion made me hesitant to proclaim too strongly that people were sinners for fear of crushing people unduly or making it impossible for them to understand that they were made in God's image. But it is possible to preserve human dignity and worth on one hand and proclaim moral failure that harms one's relationship with God on the other, even though it may take a lot of practice.

This situation is like a man I know who is one of the most beautiful, gifted and generous men I have ever met. I have always appreciated his love and unselfishness. This same individual is one of the worst husbands I have ever known. His failure to care for his wife appropriately led to a total collapse of their relationship and a legal separation. He is a beautiful and gifted man who failed in his most important human relationship. In the same way we can aggressively affirm human worth, beauty and giftedness, while still claiming that all have failed in one particular relationship—with our Creator. This is indeed a significant relationship which affects everything else, but it does not take away from the fact that all are made in God's image and loved by Him. We do not tamper with the doctrine of God's image and human worth when we address sin. We simply confess that we have failed in our relationship with God. Then, as we admit our failures, God offers us forgiveness and restores our relationship with Him because of Jesus Christ.

We need to continue to make known to the world that through faith in Christ we are given the white robes of sainthood in spite of our moral failure. Yet, it is essential for us to also make known the other side of the human paradox—that at the same time we are, and in this life always will be, sinners. A proper understanding of right doctrine in this area is essential for Christians to rightly know their position in Christ (saved by grace), and to have a healthy concern about the dangers of the old Adam and the devil. This knowledge should also help to motivate Christians to arm themselves with the Word, surround themselves with the community of believers, and partake regularly of the bread and wine.

CONCLUSION

A difficulty with discerning theological error is the very fact that its truths so often demand paradoxical thinking or require the use of distinctions. We tend to simplify ideas into either/or terms. Another difficulty is that with paradoxes and distinctions, everything stated might be true but incomplete. Consequently, we may not sense that there is error in the conclusions we arrive at.

I believe that widespread errors are occurring in the theology of many ELCA clergy because of their failure to use these tools upon which Lutheranism has always depended: paradox and distinctions. As a result, our church has become unbalanced. There is a widespread emphasis on only one side of the key paradoxes of Christian faith. Consequently, we often have an unhealthy focus on the first person of the Trinity, the sainthood of the believer and the humanity of Jesus.

Likewise, distinctions are so often unused thus blurring certain truths. Grace is only imagined as that which indiscriminately falls on believers and unbelievers alike, whether it is the grace that gives provision or the grace that justifies. Technical (theological) language can easily become the only language we use, and thus we lose our ability to call the lost and unrepentant to saving faith through psychological language. Salvation is more frequently viewed as depending on baptism alone instead of on both baptism and an ongoing, repentant faith. The Word is proclaimed as Gospel only, losing the power it can only fully achieve when preceded by the law.

Theology is always distorted when paradoxes and distinctions are ignored or misunderstood. And yet, proper thinking about the faith cannot be done without these great tools. Much of the present thinking in our denomination, and the lack of lively, life-changing faith, can be traced to this failure.

To regain our balance, we need to again listen to those who have gone before us and who have communicated to us the necessary keys to understanding our lives before God. To be confessional is to admit that on our own we cannot clearly understand theology. We have to stand on the shoulders of those who, throughout the centuries, have continued to affirm the truths that bear witness to the Scriptures, helping us to see clearly. If we choose not to do these things, we will wander in half-truths and incomplete reasoning. However, if we will again trust the Scriptures and the confessions of Lutherans who have preceded us, our church will once again become balanced and healthy, able to effectively carry on its service in power and with the Spirit's leading.

NOTES

1. Theodore G. Tappert, ed., *The Book of Concord* (Philadelphia: Fortress, 1981), 67.
2. Tappert, 78.
3. Tappert, 213.
4. Tappert, 214.
5. Tappert, 32.
6. Tappert, 35.
7. Tappert, 446.
8. Tappert, 446.
9. Tappert, 329.
10. Tappert, 228.
11. Tappert 182.
12. Tappert, 160.
13. Tappert, 137.
14. Tappert, 621.
15. Tappert, 585.
16. Tappert, 556.
17. Tappert, 555.
18. Tappert, 555.
19. Tappert, 532.
20. Tappert, 160.
21. Tappert, 165.
22. Tappert, 165.
23. Tappert, 445.
24. Tappert, 442.
25. Tappert, 440.
26. Tappert, 441.
27. Tappert, 484.
28. Tappert, 454.
29. Tappert, 521.
30. Tappert, 546.
31. Tappert, 470.
32. Tappert, 521.
33. Tappert, 521-22.
34. Tappert, 529.

35. Tappert, 533.
36. Tappert, 345.
37. Tappert, 31.
38. Tappert, 30.
39. Jaroslav Pelikan, ed., *Luther's Works*: 13 (St. Louis: Concordia; 1956), 77.
40. Pelikan, 79.
41. Pelikan, 77.
42. Pelikan, 79.
43. Pelikan, 79.
44. Pelikan, 83.
45. Pelikan, 83.
46. Tappert, 108.
47. Tappert, 144.
48. Tappert, 163.
49. Tappert, 189.
50. Tappert, 304.
51. Tappert, 560.
52. Tappert, 560.
53. Tappert, 561.
54. Jim Klobuchar, *Pursued By Grace* (Minneapolis: Fortress, 1998).
55. Pelikan, 76.
56. Tappert, 345.
57. Tappert, 526-27.
58. Tappert, 527.
59. Tappert, 549-50.
60. Presbyterian Church USA, *A Declaration of Faith* (PCUSA, 1985), 5.
61. Tappert, 27-28.
62. Tappert, 29-30.
63. Tappert, 458.
64. Tappert, 455.
65. Tappert, 433-34.
66. Tappert, 374.
67. Tappert, 378-79.
68. Tappert, 360.
69. Tappert, 543.
70. Tappert, 572.